Craft Your Own Adventure

The Deepest Cave

An Unofficial Minecraft Book

By,

DR. BLOCK

ISBN: 978-1-951728-98-4

Credits: The Warden graphics are thanks to GabrielDja's warden rig for Minemator. He's got a YouTube channel, *https://www.youtube.com/channel/UCzD4VAatib6cnjils-Quu]g*, so be sure to check it out. All other illustrations were created by Dr. Block using Minemator or are edited screenshots from Minecraft 1.18.

Published by
Eclectic Esquire Media, LLC
P.O. Box 235094
Encinitas, CA 92023-5094

Inquiries and information: *drblockbooks@gmail.com.*

Table of Contents

How to Use This Book

Welcome.

If you've never read a "choose your path" book, let me explain how to use it. As you read this book, you will be presented with directions or a series of choices at the end of each section. You then follow the directions or select one choice and turn to the page as directed. Then, you continue reading.

The important thing is not to peek at any pages other than the pages you have chosen to read. Otherwise, you might see some of the surprises in the book.

Eventually, you will come to the end of your story. Perhaps you will poof or perhaps you will complete the adventure and achieve wealth or glory.

To begin the adventure, turn to page one, which is entitled "Start Here."

Start Here

You feel the sun on your eyes, acting as a natural alarm clock. When you constructed your home base, you oriented the house specifically for this purpose. Yeah, you admit it, you are a nerd. You put a window on the eastern side of the house, facing the rising sun. You positioned your bed so the sun's rays would strike your eyes a few minutes after the sun rose. You are smart, and you know it.

By waking up the moment the sun rises, you gain a few more minutes of daylight compared to your less clever friends living in the Overworld. This has enabled you to mine just a bit more raw material each day. After three weeks in this world, it has added up.

Your home base is amazing, if you say so yourself. You've built three stories above ground and two stories hidden below ground. That's where you store your loot in well-organized chests. So far, you have an almost endless supply of food, hundreds of torches, and raw materials of almost every kind. You haven't found much copper yet and still haven't been to the Nether to search for ancient debris. Those are the two highest-priority items on your "to do" list: locate copper and upgrade your diamond armor and weapons to netherite.

Today, you hope to cross one of those items off your list. You are planning to explore a cave system you discovered yesterday with the goal of locating a large copper deposit. You want to put a copper roof on your house. You can't wait to watch it age and see the patina of green slowly creep across it until your entire roof has an elegant, aged appearance.

You get out of bed and eat a small breakfast of a loaf of bread and a chicken leg to top up your hunger bar. After clearing the kitchen table, you descend into your subterranean storage area. You walk to the armor stand and equip your diamond armor. No enchantments yet, but that has mattered little. You select a plethora of weapons and tools to bring on your expedition, including two diamond swords, three pickaxes (two diamond, one iron), a half dozen buckets (two filled with water), and a few potions of healing.

You double check your supplies, nodding to yourself when you confirm you've packed everything you think you will need. You step out of your house and shut the door. You smile when you see your small farming operation. You plan to expand it eventually, but for now, you don't mind hunting for most of your food.

You consult your map. There is a village on the way to the cave. You decide to stop there to see if you can make some decent trades before getting to the cave.

Turn the page.

After walking for about ten minutes, you arrive at the local village. You'd considered locating your house closer to the village, but you find villagers annoying, so you wanted some distance between you and the village. You have plans to wall off the village someday and make the villagers work exclusively for your benefit, but for now, you let them live with the illusion of freedom.

You enter the village and see two villagers wandering the street. One is a master farmer; the other is a journeyman fletcher. Which one do you want to trade with?

To trade with the master farmer, turn to page 4.

To trade with the journeyman fletcher, turn to page 5.

If you just want to pass through the village without trading, turn to page 8.

You head toward the master farmer. You are hopeful he might have some good trades. You are looking for something rare. You aren't a noob anymore, so you can easily craft the basic items of this world yourself.

You approach the farmer and smile. He smiles back, but says nothing. Instead, he opens his offer book and holds it in front of you. You appreciate his no nonsense approach to trades. So many villagers want to make small talk. It is one of the things that makes them so annoying.

You review the offered trades. *Ah, there is something I want*, you think.

You point at the picture of a golden carrot. The master farmer nods. "Three emeralds," he says.

You consider it a bargain and gladly hand over the emeralds. You plan to use the golden carrot to help tame a horse. You haven't tamed any animals yet and wanted to start with a horse and then tame a dog.

The villager takes your emeralds and hands over the golden carrot. You smile and tuck it into your inventory. The master farmer wanders away.

If you want to trade with the journeyman fletcher, turn to page 7.

If you are done trading and want to leave the village, turn to page 11.

You walk toward the fletcher. He sees you coming his way and rubs his hands together. When you are within speaking distance, he cracks a wide smile.

"Ah, valiant player. How can I be of service?"

"Stop trying to sweet talk me," you say with a scowl. "Just show me what you got."

The fletcher bows. "Very well. The customer is always right—except about price, of course."

You roll your eyes. The fletcher removes his offer book. You see what is available. Most of the trades are pretty weak until you spot it: a crossbow. You don't have one of those yet.

"How much for the crossbow?"

The fletcher smiles and nods. "The crossbow is easily worth five emeralds, but for you, hurrr, you can have it for three."

Three seems expensive, but it's easier than having to poof a pillager and hope he drops a crossbow. You rub your chin and then nod. "Yeah, okay."

You hand over the emeralds and the villager gives you the crossbow. You turn and walk away.

If you want to trade with the master farmer, turn to page 6.

If you are done trading and want to leave the village, turn to page 11.

Now that you are done with the journeyman fletcher, you head toward the master farmer. You are hopeful he might have some good trades. You are looking for something rare. You aren't a noob anymore, so you can easily get the basic items of this world yourself.

You approach the farmer and smile. He smiles back, but says nothing. Instead, he opens his offer book and holds it in front of you. You appreciate his no nonsense approach to trades. So many villagers want to make small talk. It is one of the things that makes them so annoying.

You review the offered trades. *Ah, there is something I want*, you think.

You point at the picture of a golden carrot. The master farmer nods. "Three emeralds," he says.

You consider it a bargain and gladly hand over the emeralds. You plan to use the golden carrot to help tame a horse. You haven't tamed any animals yet and wanted to start with a horse and then tame a dog.

The villager takes your emeralds and hands over the golden carrot. You smile and tuck it into your inventory. The master farmer wanders away, and you depart from the village.

Turn to page 11.

The golden carrot is pretty awesome, but maybe the fletcher has something cool too. You walk toward the fletcher. He sees you coming his way and rubs his hands together. When you are within speaking distance, he cracks a wide smile.

"Ah, valiant player. How can I be of service?"

"Stop trying to sweet talk me," you say with a scowl. "Just show me what you got."

The fletcher bows. "Very well. The customer is always right—except about price, of course."

You roll your eyes. The fletcher removes his offer book. You see what is available. Most of the trades are pretty weak until you spot it: a crossbow. You don't have one of those yet.

"How much for the crossbow?"

The fletcher smiles and nods. "The crossbow is easily worth five emeralds, but for you, hurrr, you can have it for three."

Three seems expensive, but it's cheaper than having to poof a pillager and hope he drops a crossbow. You rub your chin and then nod. "Yeah, okay."

You hand over the emeralds and the villager gives you the crossbow. You turn and walk away.

Turn to page 11.

As you stare at the two villagers—who've now spotted you and are making a bee-line in your direction—you change your mind. You don't want to trade with any villagers today. You just want to get to the cave.

You turn and dash away from the villagers and get to the outskirts of town. You breathe a sigh of relief as you put some distance between you and the village. But then, it happens: a wandering trader and his two llamas appear as though from nowhere.

"Would you like to make a trade?" the wandering trader asks, bowing obsequiously.

"No, I would not," you say, moving to the side to get around the trader.

"But, sir, I have some lovely mushrooms, seeds, and flowers for your selection."

"Get lost," you say, shoving the wandering trader so hard that he nearly falls down.

His llamas interpret your lack of consumer sentiment to be an attack on their master. They both spit on you. Their spit globs smack you in the face, causing two hearts of total damage. You couldn't care less about the damage. It's the nasty, sticky, smelly spit on your face that really bothers you.

"Please accept my apologies, sir," the wandering trader says, trying to ease the situation. "Now, about that trade...."

The wandering trader clearly did not understand the meaning of your shove, and his llamas are just plain nasty. You consider blowing them all up with a TNT block.

If you ignite a TNT block, turn to page 10.

If you leave the wandering trader and continue toward the cave, turn to page 11.

You can feel your face flushing with anger. You reach into your inventory, grab a TNT block, and toss it on the ground. You quickly ignite it with a flint and steel and then run away.

The wandering trader moves to come after you, but his llamas try to pull him in the other direction. They are doomed.

A few seconds pass and then *KA-DOOooom!* The TNT explodes.

You turn around and grin. There is a massive hole in the ground and no sign of the wandering trader and his llamas.

Turn to page 11.

You are happy to be alone. A well-worn dirt road winds for quite some distance beyond the village. You follow it until it begins to narrow and then disappears into a grassy meadow. You take a deep breath and exhale, enjoying the peaceful landscape.

A few minutes later, when you have nearly crossed the meadow, you notice some spiders skittering underneath the nearby trees. You are thankful they are peaceful during the day. You don't like spiders very much. Now that you have more powerful weapons and armor, you are able to poof them without too much difficulty. But you remember your first few days and nights in this world. You scowl thinking about how many spiders made you poof and respawn, delaying your progress and acquisition of goods.

You think about making some of these spiders poof, in part for revenge and in part to collect drops. It will delay you getting to the cave, but it might be fun.

If you attack the spiders in the woods, turn to page 12.
If you continue on, turn to page 13.

You rush toward the spiders in the woods. When you are close enough, you see there are three of them. No problem. Plus, since it is daytime, they will be passive until you attack the first one. Easy peasy.

You walk until you are standing next to one of the spiders and then slash it with all your strength. A single blow and it is already flashing red. You finish it off as the other two spiders charge you.

You take a defensive stance. The spiders land a couple of blows, but it doesn't take long before you make each of them poof.

You gather one spider eye and three strings from their drop piles. Your lust for revenge satisfied, you move on.

Turn to page 13.

As you continue on your journey to the cave, you arrive at a familiar location. There is a stand of three large trees growing in the middle of a plain. You look to the right and see the beginnings of a swamp biome. To the left are hills and mountains. You consult your map.

In order to get to the cave you want to explore, you can take one of two routes: you can take a shortcut through the swamp or take the longer, more scenic route through the mountains. Although the swamp will save considerable time, you know that a vicious, evil witch lives in the swamp. You've always hated witches, but you want to get to the cave as soon as possible. The shortcut sounds attractive to you. On the other hand, a nice stroll through the mountains might do you good. You've always loved the mountains.

If you go through the swamp, turn to page 14.

If you begin climbing the mountains, turn to page 25.

You enter the swamp. The dank air assaults your nostrils, but you'll get used to it soon. Besides, this is a shortcut, remember?

Your feet squish in the soft ground near the murky swamp water. You hear the *glub glub* of bubbles popping through the muddy shoreline close by. You take a few more careful steps and then you hear something you've never heard before: "Croak. Croak."

You turn in the direction of the sound, which is coming from the water. You stare and see strange brown and green creatures resting on the tops of several lily pads. *What are these things?* You reach for your sword, just in case the creatures turn out to be hostile.

One of them hops off a lily pad. It swims through the water and then scrambles onto land. It stares at you with its bulgy eyes. "Ribbit," it says.

You laugh. It reminds you of an ugly axolotl. Then you remember—it's a frog. You heard another player talking about them one night when you were attending a PVP contest in a distant city. You move toward it to get a closer look when it suddenly shoots its tongue out of its mouth. The sticky tip of the tongue lands on the flat of your sword and starts pulling it away from you!

If you try to yank your sword away from the frog, turn to page 15.

If you slash at the frog with your sword, turn to page 16.

You are dumbfounded at the strength in the frog's tongue. You yank on your sword, trying to pull it away, but can't seem to get it loose.

You think: *How can something so small be so overpowered?*

You dig your heels into the soft ground and, using all your strength, yank the sword again. Finally, the tongue breaks free and snaps back into the frog's mouth. The frog scowls at you, but then hops back into the water.

Turn to page 17.

You sneer at the frog. "Let go of my sword!" you demand. The frog can't understand you and probably doesn't care what you think.

You growl and rush toward the frog, its tongue still attached to the sword. As the tongue gets some slack in it, you raise your sword into the air and prepare to deliver a death blow.

The frog's eyes go wide. It may not have much intelligence, but it knows a rage-filled player when it sees one. The frog's tongue immediately detaches from the sword and snaps back into its mouth.

"Oh, no you don't," you growl.

You bring your diamond sword down toward the defenseless frog. But just before the sword would have cut the frog in half, it uses its powerful legs to launch itself into the air. Your sword sweeps harmlessly through the air and then its tip is buried in the mucky ground.

"Netherrack!" you curse as you pull your sword from the ground and clean it with some wool.

The frog meanwhile has landed on top of a lily pad. You hear a chorus of "croaks" and "ribbits." You can't be certain, but you think the frogs are laughing at you.

As you put your sword back into your inventory, you sneer at the colony of frogs. Time to move on.

Turn to page 17.

"Stupid frog," you mutter as you walk away from the edge of the water.

You've decided to head for a group of oak trees. You assume the ground will be harder, making travel easier. If you keep as much as possible to the ground where trees grow, you should get through this swamp much more quickly.

As you walk through the stand of oak trees, you admire the vines dangling toward the ground. You hear a rustling and notice a pig rutting around nearby, probably searching for some mushrooms to eat. For a moment, you think about killing the pig for food, but you've got plenty of food in your inventory and don't want to waste any more time. You really want to start exploring that cave.

A few minutes later, you hear rustling coming from behind a nearby tree. It's loud. Your heart starts pounding.

Is it the witch?

You've fought a witch once before. It didn't end well. You're thinking it might be best to run away. But you have diamond armor now, a powerful sword, and a bow with many quivers of arrows. The last time you fought a witch, you only had leather armor and an iron sword. You didn't even have a bow and arrows.

If you stay to see what is causing the rustling, turn to page 18.

If you run away, turn to page 20.

You aren't a noob anymore, so you aren't going to run like a noob. Noobs are cowards. You are an experienced player. Eventually, you intend to dominate this world. If you let yourself run from every noise you hear, you are no better than a chicken or a cow.

You turn to face the trees from which the rustling is coming. You arm yourself with a bow and arrows. You nock an arrow and pull back on the string, ready to attack.

The rustling is coming closer. It's definitely something large. It could be a witch, but it might also be an armored zombie or armored skeleton surviving in the daylight.

You hear branches crunching. Whatever it is, it's about to reveal itself....

When you see the source of the noise, you shake your head and chuckle. You lower your weapon. It's a villager. When he stumbles into the clearing in which you are standing, he startles.

"What are you doing here?" he asks.

"I was about to ask you the same question," you say. "There aren't any villages nearby."

"I've lived in the swamp since I spawned," he says. "Would you care to trade?"

"How much would you charge for information?"

The villager shrugs. "Tell me what you want to know, and I'll give you a price."

"I'm trying to avoid the witch who lives in this swamp. Do you know where her hut is?"

The villager grins. "I do. And I'll tell you that information for, hurrr, ten emeralds."

The price is so ridiculous, you laugh out loud. But you're in a hurry and, let's face it, you're pretty rich. You dig into your inventory and toss the ten emeralds to the feet of the swap villager. The villager crouches and slowly picks up the emeralds. After he laboriously tucks them one by one into his own inventory, he smiles at you.

"The witch's hut is on the other side of the swamp. Unless she's in these parts gathering potion supplies, I doubt you will encounter her."

You smile. "Great. Thanks."

"Would you care to trade for anything else?"

"Get lost," you say as you turn your back on the villager. You resume your travels toward the cave.

Turn to page 37.

You turn and run.

Every battle is a risk, and you don't want to fight today if you don't have to. You want to explore the cave and obtain stacks of copper ore so you can build your awesome roof. If you're lucky, you'll also find amethyst crystals and be able to craft one of those spy glasses you've heard about.

You run toward a gap between two oak trees. As you run, you glance over your shoulder to make sure whatever was making that noise isn't following you. It's not.

You turn back around and spot the gap. Just a few more strides and you'll be home free.

You sprint through the gap. It is surprisingly dark. You look up and see the canopy of the oak trees is thick. You worry it might be thick enough that nighttime mobs have survived in this area. You spot another gap and charge ahead.

As you enter the second gap, you glance over your shoulder, checking again to make sure you aren't being followed. As you turn around, you smash into someone....

Turn the page.

You crumple to the ground. Your head is spinning.

It takes a couple of seconds, but you are finally able to lift your head and search the area. Whatever you hit, it was your size. You rub your head and then see movement to your right.

A clump of grass obscures your vision. You can't quite see who or what you hit. And, then, you see a splash potion bottle arc into the sky, followed by a malevolent cackle. The witch! You collided with the witch!

Turn the page.

You roll to the side. The splash potion impacts the ground where you had been a moment ago. You fumble for your bow and arrows. That moment of attention to your inventory costs you. A splash potion of poison smashes against your chest.

The pain is instantaneous. Your health begins to decrease rapidly. You groan, but manage to get an arrow in your bow. You aim at the witch and fire.

The arrow hits home. The witch screams and then throws another splash potion at you. As you see the bottle speeding through the air, you realize it is a slowness potion. If that hits you, you could be done for. You dive to the side and narrowly avoid the potion.

The witch cackles again. She reaches into her robe for yet another potion.

You think you can take her out, but you worry you might poof. Even if the witch doesn't kill you, she might weaken you so much that a lowly slime might come out of nowhere and finish the job. All you wanted to do was explore a cave, not battle swamp witches. You realize you have two options: run away, or stand and fight and hope for the best.

If you run, turn to page 23.
If you fight, turn to page 24.

You have your pride, but you aren't stupid. Today is not about fighting; today is about exploring. You tuck away your bow and arrow and run.

"Coward!" the witch shouts, taunting you as you flee.

You glance over your shoulders several times to make sure she does not follow you. Mercifully, she does not.

You slow down, but keep walking at a quick pace. You want to get out of this swamp as soon as possible. Your shortcut hasn't saved you as much time as you'd hoped.

Another twenty minutes pass before you reach the edge of the swamp. A large mountain looms in front of you. About thirty blocks up from the base of the mountain you see it, the black opening to the cave.

Turn page 37.

You growl at the witch. You launch an arrow at her, hitting her dead center in the chest. The witch staggers.

You drop your bow and pull your sword as you charge the witch. She pulls a splash potion of slowness. But before she can throw it at you, you reach her. You slash savagely with your sword. The witch begins to flash red.

You slash one last time. But, before your sword finds home, the witch manages to hit you with the splash potion. You watch as your sword hits the witch and she poofs, but then you feel the slowness effect take hold.

You only have four hearts left. Thank goodness you don't need to fight anymore. But then, you see it: a chicken jockey.

No!

The chicken jockey darts toward you. You try to slash it with your sword, but the slowness effect is too strong. The jockey lands a blow with its own sword. Three of your hearts vanish.

Only. One. Heart. Left.

You face the chicken jockey bravely, but its speed is too much. It crashes into you again and … you poof.

If you want to go back and make a different decision, turn to page 22.

If you want to start this story over at the beginning, turn to page 1.

You despise witches, especially after meeting one when you were a noob. That didn't end well. Just thinking about that embarrassing situation makes your blood boil. You don't mind spending an extra hour or two going over the mountains where it is safer.

You begin climbing the mountains. It's easy at first, with gentle slopes and even a small meadow here and there. Soon, however, the terrain steepens, and you begin to curse your decision. At least the swamp would have been flat, if more dangerous. Too late to change now, you continue on.

You are about one-third of the way to your destination when you summit the first, snow-capped peak. You glance to the side and see that there is a beautiful view.

If you stay and admire the view, turn to page 26.

If you ignore the view and keep moving, turn to page 34.

You've been making good time on your journey so far, so you think a brief rest to admire the view is well worth it.

You turn and look at the valley below. The crisp, clear air lets you see for miles. You can see the mountains as they slope down into the flatlands. You can even see the village near your home base. You realize that this is a great vantage point, and the sheer cliff just in front of your feet means you could make this position very secure. You might come back one day and build a small base here with a lookout.

As you begin scheming the layout of your future satellite base, you suddenly feel a searing pain in your rear end!

"Oof," you grunt as you are launched into the air and fall off the cliff!

As you are screaming and falling, you look back at where you had been standing. You see a goat glaring at you and snorting. Just before you impact the ground, you realize what has happened: You stood still for too long and a goat snuck up behind you and head-butted you.

A few more seconds of weightlessness and then you slam into snow at the base of the cliff. You take a lot of fall damage, but nothing you can't recover from. You stand up and shake your fist at the goat. It snorts, turns up its nose, and disappears from view.

You scowl at the goat and turn to examine your surroundings.

You are shocked to see a pillager outpost nestled in a narrow valley a short walk away. You're surprised you couldn't see it from the summit. Luckily, you don't think any pillagers have seen you.

If you approach the outpost to investigate, turn to page 28.

If you turn away and continue toward the cave, turn to page 33.

You've seen a few pillager outposts in the past, but you've always avoided them because you weren't strong enough to face them. Now, you are strong enough. You don't want to attack the outpost today, but you can do some reconnaissance and plan an attack later.

You cautiously approach the outpost until you have a clear view of it from behind a rock. You see several pillagers milling about and two iron golems trapped in a cage. You think that freeing the golems so they will assist you might be a good plan. You also realize having a tamed wolf or fox (or maybe three or four) with you could help, too.

You make a few mental notes and then sneak away. But you only get a few paces when you hear a telltale hissing sound. You turn and see a flashing creeper rushing toward you.

If you run away, turn to page 29.

If you try to kill it with your sword before it explodes, turn to page 30.

You aren't sure how the creeper got so close before you noticed it. You feel like a noob. Normally, you'd stand your ground, but you still haven't recovered entirely from your fall damage and worry that maybe the creeper explosion might be enough to cause you to poof.

Thankfully, the creeper can't catch up with you.

You begin climbing the mountains again, eager to get to the cave.

Turn to page 34.

"Stupid creeper," you mutter as you pull your diamond sword.

The creeper charges toward you. You slash at it as quickly as you can. The creeper is flashing faster now. Is it going to explode?

Poof.

You breathe a sigh of relief as the creeper vanishes in a puff of smoke, leaving a pile of gunpowder. You pick up the gunpowder.

As you are adding the gunpowder to the rest of the gunpowder stored in your inventory, you notice movement out of the corner of your eye. Three creepers! They spot you and charge.

If you stand and fight, turn to page 31.

If you run, turn to page 32.

Ok, if you insist. Um, how should I put this? I guess I'll just say it: You made a terrible decision.

The three creepers charge you and begin to flash. You manage to poof one of them, but the other two explode right next to you.

You poof.

If you want to respawn to the prior page and make a different decision, turn to page 30.

If you want to start this book at the beginning, turn to page 1.

Discretion is the better part of valor, as they say. You dart away from the three creepers. You are out of their line of sight quickly, and they do not pursue you.

It is time to get back on the path to the cave. You pull out your map to confirm your location. Then, you turn in the correct direction and begin climbing the mountains again.

Turn to page 34.

You look back up at the snowcapped mountains. If only that goat hadn't shoved you off that cliff, you'd be nearly to the cave by now. You grind your teeth with frustration.

You scan the foothills and see what looks like an easy trail to get back to the ridgeline where travel will be fastest—as long as you avoid any more goat catastrophes.

You trudge to the trail and climb back up to the ridgeline.

Turn to page 34.

You walk along the mountaintops admiring the view, but not stopping in any place for too long, wary of head-butting goats.

At one point, a group of three rabbits emerges from behind a spruce tree. You think about harvesting them for food, but rabbits can be annoying and difficult to catch. You decide to ignore them.

About thirty minutes pass, and you begin to descend the mountains, entering a biome with patchy snow and a lot more trees. As you travel through this biome, you spot two foxes frolicking in a meadow.

"No way," you gasp. You remember that if you can breed two wild foxes, the baby will trust you. You've always wanted a fox as a pet. You even have enough sweet berries in your inventory.

You approach the foxes slowly, careful not to scare them. When you are close enough, you reach into your inventory for the sweet berries.

Blip!

Before you can pull out the berries, a wandering trader and his llama team appear almost on top of the foxes! They scatter.

The wandering trader smiles at you. "Would you like to trade?"

If you ignore the trader and resume your journey, turn to page 35.

If you mercilessly attack the wandering trader, turn to page 36.

"Get lost, loser," you say as you push past the wandering trader.

"But, sir," he says, calling after you. "I have amazing trades. I have fresh buckets of fish and beetroots seeds."

You hunch your shoulders and keep walking.

"What about pumpkin seeds and sand?"

This guy is getting on your nerves. You turn our back on him and start walking toward your final destination.

"Please, noble player. Won't you trade with me?"

If you change your mind and decide to attack the wandering trader, turn to page 36.

If you continue walking away, turn to page 37.

It is brutal. The wandering trader has no chance. The llamas just stand there and stare as their master poofs.

You glare at the two animals. "You want some of this?"

The llamas' eyes go wide. They snort and quickly turn and wander away.

You tuck your sword away and resume your travels.

Turn to page 37.

It took longer than expected, but you've finally arrived near the entrance to the cave. The dark entrance yawns before you. From where you stand, about twenty blocks in front of the cave, it appears as though the cave immediately descends into the earth.

You approach the cave and look inside. You were correct. There is a steep descent. You ignite a torch and enter the cave.

You take about thirty steps when you come to a wide rock landing. From this location, the cave appears to split into three passages. The passages to the left and right are both dark and mysterious. The passage immediately in front of you seems to emit a hint of light, as though something were glowing inside or perhaps many torches are near.

If you take the dark passage to the left, turn to page 38.

If the take the glowing central passage, turn to page 58.

If you take the dark passage to the right, turn to page 70.

You look at your three options and shrug. They all probably connect at somewhere in the depths. Even if they don't, you can explore the other passages later, either tomorrow or a few weeks from now. It doesn't really matter. Your primary goal is to get copper and make an awesome roof for your home base.

You decide to enter the passage on the left. You raise your torch high and proceed.

It begins with a narrow passage, maybe four blocks wide. You wonder if it will open into a massive cavern or if it will stay narrow or even reach a dead end. You continue through the narrow passage for a few minutes, placing torches as needed to mark your path and to prevent mobs from spawning. From time to time, you stop to mine any easily accessible ores, mostly coal, but no copper yet.

Finally, after five minutes, the passage begins to widen. Just ahead, you notice a cavern branching to the left of the main passage. You cautiously approach and ready your sword.

The area to the left is more of a pocket chamber than a side passage. You raise your torch and see its light reflecting off something purple. Amethyst! Even though you are hoping to find copper, you could use amethyst for decoration and for a spyglass.

You pull your diamond pickaxe from your inventory and smash an amethyst cluster. It vanishes and drops ... nothing.

"What?" you gasp. You tap your chin as you stare at the space where the amethyst cluster had been a moment ago.

Then you remember. You need silk touch in order to mine amethyst effectively. Of course, you don't have any pickaxes with that enchantment with you. Worse, your enchanting table is at home.

"What a noob," you mutter. You kick the ground.

And that's when you hear it: the clattering of bones.

You turn around and see three skeletons, one with an iron helmet and chest plate, standing in front of the only exit to the chamber.

You switch from your pickaxe to your diamond sword. As you do that, two arrows embed in your diamond chest plate. The impact is painful, but the diamond armor keeps the damage low.

You rush forward, slashing at the two unarmored skeletons first. It doesn't take long to make them poof, but you continue taking damage. About one-third of your health is gone when you turn to the armored skeleton.

The skeleton sneers at you with a toothless, malevolent grin. When you look into his empty eye sockets, you feel a shiver down your spine. You lunge for the skeleton just as one of his arrows hits your shin. You howl in pain, but that doesn't stop you. You surge forward and soon put an end to the skeleton.

In the aftermath of the fight, you see three arrows and two bones floating. You walk through them and add them to your inventory.

That wasn't so hard, you think as you take a deep breath and step out of the room.

BRRrrrr.

You spin around and see a zombie lurching toward you. The zombie is standing on the path where you came from. You can easily avoid it by running the other way, which is the way you want to go.

If you flee to safety, turn to page 41.
If you flee to safety, turn to page 41.
If you fight the zombie, turn to page 42.

As much as you want to make the zombie poof, you decide you can do that on the way out of the cave if the zombie is stupid enough to be waiting for you.

"See you later, dork," you say with a grin as you turn and run.

The zombie moans, sounding sad that it didn't get an opportunity to make you poof.

Turn to page 45.

You stride toward the hapless zombie. "I'm so sick of zombies," you say before slashing at it a few times and watching it poof. You ignore the piece of rotten flesh it dropped.

BRRrrrr. BRRrrrr. BRRrrrr.

Your body is suddenly covered with goosebumps. You turn around and see three zombies lurching toward you. They are blocking the path to descend into the cave.

"Where did those come from?" you say. You don't get an answer. You consider running away, back to the cave entrance, when you hear: *BRRrrrr. BRRrrrr.*

You turn around. Two more zombies, one of which is wearing a golden helmet, are lurching toward you, passing the rotten flesh drop from the first zombie.

You're surrounded. You can only think of two options. You can stand your ground and fight, or you can mine straight down and hope for the best.

If you mine straight down, turn to page 43.
If you stand and fight, turn to page 44.

You know it's risky to mine straight down, but you're pretty sure you'll poof if you stay here. You pull your pickaxe and swiftly begin clearing blocks from beneath your feet.

Three blocks. Four blocks. Five blocks—

"Aaaaaaaahhhhhhh," you scream as you fall through the hole.

Your arms flail, but you maintain your grip on the pickaxe. As you fall through the air, you examine your surroundings. You've fallen into a dripstone cave! You look down and see that you are going to splat on the ground.

But, there is a lake just a few blocks to the side. You manage to kick a stalactite hanging from the ceiling of the chamber. This redirects you to the edge of the lake and you splash in the water, taking minimal fall damage.

You stand up, thankful to be alive, and take a few steps through the water before reaching the shore. As you stand there, drying off, you survey the cave.

You marvel at the dozens of stalactites and stalagmites, some of which have been dripping for so long that they have fused into stout columns. As you wander along the shore of the underground lake, you notice a glow squid swimming in the water.

If you ignore the glow squid and keep walking, turn to page 46.

If you would like to harvest the glow squid, turn to page 47.

The odds aren't in your favor, but you aren't going to run from some wimpy zombies. You manage to make two of them poof, but their numbers are too much.

The last three surround you, making it difficult for you to get a full swing with your sword. The zombies punch and bite you. Soon, you're flashing red.

You switch from your sword to your pickaxe and try to escape by mining straight down. But, it's too late.

You poof.

If you'd like to respawn on the prior page and make a different decision, turn to page 42.

If you'd like to start over at the beginning of this book, turn to page 1.

You continue exploring the cave for another twenty minutes without incident. You spy some hostile mobs in a massive chamber below you, but they are too far away to be any concern. Besides, it doesn't seem like the path you are on will take you to that chamber. Instead, your path leads you into another narrow passage.

You hurry through the uninteresting passage, placing torches here and there. The narrow passage continues for several hundred paces until it opens into a large dripstone cave.

You don't see any hostile mobs yet, so you enter the chamber. You marvel at the dozens of stalactites and stalagmites, some of which have been dripping for so long that they have fused into stout columns. As you wander along the shore of the underground lake, you notice a glow squid swimming in the water.

If you ignore the glow squid and keep walking, turn to page 46.

If you would like to harvest the glow squid, turn to page 47.

You consider harvesting the squid, but you've already got plenty of glow squid ink sacs back home. You ignore the glow squid, but keep an eye out for copper. You've heard that copper deposits in dripstone caves can be larger than in most other locations.

You continue wandering around the cave, gazing at its wondrous geologic formations. And then, you see it. A massive copper vein. Your eyes widen and you run to it.

You yank your pickaxe from your inventory. You harvest with abandon, eventually collecting forty-two blocks of copper ore. You wish there was more, but this should be a good start for your copper roof.

You explore some more and find a few smaller copper deposits and mine those. You've got sixty-two blocks now. It seems like you've mined all the available copper. You are happy.

If you'd like to return home and craft your roof, turn to page 144.

If you'd like to continue exploring deeper into the cave, turn to page 48.

You wait until the glow squid drifts close to shore and then you slash at it with your sword. The squid tries to escape by moving to the right along the shore.

"Stupid squid," you say, taunting it. "Try swimming away from the shore if you want to survive."

You slash at the squid again, and then you hear a massive *crack!* It seems like it came from above you.

You turn to look, just as the point of a massive stalactite impales you.

You poof.

If you'd like to respawn and ignore the glow squid, turn to page 46.

If you'd like to start over from the beginning, turn to page 1.

You notice a small opening on the other side of the dripstone cave. It looks like the start of a passage. You walk toward it. You notice a cave spider in the distance, too far to be a threat. Nevertheless, you begin to jog toward the opening.

When you arrive, you look into the opening. You confirm your suspicions; this passage leads deeper into the depths of the cave.

You enter the passage and travel without incident for nearly ten minutes. Finally, the passage narrows to an opening slightly larger than the size of a door. You step through and find yourself on a small ledge overlooking a dark abyss. At the edge of the ledge is a steep staircase, only a single block wide. It is the only way off the ledge other than returning the way you came.

That's when you notice the small stone sign at the top of the stairs. You move closer and read it.

"Great treasure awaits, but only for those who can avoid certain death."

You aren't sure whether to believe the sign or roll your eyes. Most likely it is just some player trying to prevent anyone else from discovering something super amazing at the bottom of the stairs. Still, you've heard of a monster who lurks at the bottom of caves. Maybe that is what the sign means by "certain death"?

If you heed the warning and decide to return home, turn to page 144.

If you ignore the warning and continue, turn to page 50.

You travel without incident for nearly ten minutes. Finally, the passage you are following narrows to an opening slightly larger than the size of a door. You step through and find yourself on a small ledge. At the edge of the ledge is a steep staircase, only a single block wide. It is the only way off the ledge other than returning the way you came.

That's when you notice the small stone sign at the top of the stairs. You move closer and read it.

"Great treasure awaits, but only for those who can avoid certain death."

You aren't sure whether to believe the sign or roll your eyes. Most likely it is just some player trying to prevent anyone else from discovering something super amazing at the bottom of the stairs. Still, you've heard of a monster who lurks at the bottom of caves. Maybe that is what the sign means by "certain death"?

If you heed the warning and decide to return home, turn to page 144.

If you ignore the warning and continue, turn to page 50.

You aren't a noob. Some vague sign doesn't scare you.

You descend the narrow, precarious staircase. On either side, there is a deep drop. You aren't sure how deep because everything is pitch dark. You consider dropping a torch over the edge, but worry that some griefer might have made a massive pile of TNT down there just waiting for some fool to drop a torch on it.

About thirty steps down, you arrive at a ten block by five block landing. In one corner of the landing, you see a single amethyst shard. You reach for it, but pause before you touch it. You realize how weird it is that you tried to get amethyst earlier but couldn't, and now a single shard is waiting for you. Seems like it might be a trap. Still, if you grab the shard, you'll be able to craft a spyglass as soon as you get home.

If you pick up the amethyst shard, turn to page 51.

If you ignore the shard and continue descending the stairs, turn to page 57.

You place two torches on the landing so you have plenty of light. You grip your diamond sword tightly and walk toward the floating shard. When your body comes into contact with it, the shard is absorbed into your inventory.

You breathe a sigh of relief. *No trap.* But, your relief is short-lived.

You hear a whistling sound and then a firework explodes to the right of the landing. You cover your eyes and cower.

What is going on?!?

Suddenly, you hear a scream and then footsteps. You take your hand away from your eyes and see a player, dressed head-to-toe in netherite armor, charging up from the depths. His eyes are crazed. He means to make you poof.

If you flee up the stairs, turn to page 52.

If you stand your ground and fight, turn to page 53

You've had enough fighting for today. You are going to get away from this maniac and get as far away from this cave as possible.

You toss a couple of cobblestone blocks behind you and charge up the stairs. You look over your shoulder. The cobblestone seems to have done what you intended: slowed down your pursuer.

You've climbed about halfway back to the top when a zombie lurches out of the darkness. Oh, no! You stop and slash at it, but the zombie grabs your arm and pulls you off the stairs. The two of you plummet into the abyss.

There is nothing you can do to escape. You fall to your doom and poof.

If you want to respawn on the prior page, turn to page 51.

If you want to start at the beginning, turn to page 1.

You realize you should have heeded the warning sign, but it is too late for second thoughts and regrets. You have just enough time to pull your crossbow and shoot the player. The crossbow bolt hits home, but seems to have little effect through the netherite armor.

Your attacker growls. "Prepare to meet your doom!" You don't like melodrama. You just want to get this over with, one way or another.

You switch to your sword and take a couple of steps down the stairs toward the onrushing player. You do not want the player getting on even ground with you. As long as you hold the high ground, you stand a chance. You slash at the player. He ducks and slashes back at you. He makes contact with your legs. Your diamond armor helps, but you receive damage.

Turn the page.

The two of you battle for nearly a minute. Your health bar is dangerously low, but you've dealt damage too. You kick the player in the chest, and he stumbles backward down the stairs. This opens enough space between the two of you to give you time to find the last remaining splash potion of harming in your inventory. You throw it at the player. It's a direct hit. He screams.

He rushes toward you. He looks completely insane. This will be the final battle. Only one of you is going home. You only have time to make one defensive move. Do you take a step back or do you duck?

If you take a step back, turn to page 55.
If you duck, turn to page 56.

You need to get away from this lunatic. You take a step back, hoping the space will allow you to avoid the blow from your attacker and ... you avoid it!

Unfortunately, you step awkwardly and slip off the stairs.

As you plummet to your doom, the player stares down at you, laughing the entire time.

If you'd like to respawn at the prior decision point, turn to page 54.

If you want to go back to the beginning of the book, turn to page 1.

You decide to duck. If the player's sword misses you, you should be able to counterattack before he can defend himself. But, you must time your move perfectly.

You wait until he swings. You fall to your knees. You feel the flat of the netherite sword scrape the top of your diamond helmet, but you don't receive any damage.

The player barely stops his momentum from carrying him over the edge of the stairs. He would have been safe, if you hadn't kicked his legs. The player stumbles, his arms wheeling, and then he falls into the abyss, plummeting to his doom.

You listen to his screams and then the distant *thump* as he impacts the bottom of the pit.

"Nice try, griefer," you say with a scowl as you ignite a new torch and continue down the stairs.

Turn the page.

The stairs continue downward for nearly one hundred steps before finally reaching level ground. You raise your torch and see only a narrow passage. You are hemmed in by walls. Unless you want to break through the walls with your pickaxe, the only way to go is forward, which is what you do.

You walk down the passage for about a minute before arriving at its end. There is an open doorway. Through the opening, you can see the flicker of candles and a blue-tinted glow.

You feel a twitch of fear, but you move forward. You've been through too much to turn back now.

Turn to page 111.

Maybe it's a bad idea, but you decide to take the central passage to investigate the glow inside. It's probably something awesome, but just in case it isn't, you pull your diamond sword.

With a torch in your off hand, you enter the passage.

As you move forward, the glow becomes brighter. You think of three possibilities: lots of torches, a hole letting in sunlight, or glow berries. You hope it's glow berries.

You only have to take about thirty steps before you get the answer. You just found a massive lush cave.

The vines growing up the sides of the cave and hanging from the ceiling are thick. Azalea flowers and glow berries abound. You greedily gather as many glow berries as you can. You plan to eat most of them, but will use others to grow more vines near your home base for decoration.

As you move further into the lush cave, you marvel at the trio of waterfalls cascading from the middle of the ceiling into an azure lake. You move closer to the lake and see at least a dozen axolotls swimming in the lake. You really want to grab an axolotl and take it back to your base. You'll build an aquarium for it.

Still, the main reason you are exploring this cave is to find copper. You shouldn't waste time. But, the axolotls are so cute!

If you try to capture an axolotl, turn to page 59.

If you leave the lush cave and move further into the depths of the cave system, turn to page 65.

You remove an empty bucket from your inventory and, while standing at a distance from the group of axolotls, fill it with lake water. You creep along the shore toward where the axolotls are swimming.

You see axolotls of all colors, except the ultra-rare blue variant. *Oh, well,* you think, *maybe you'll get a blue one someday.* You decide to capture a pink one since those are the cutest.

You lean over with the bucket hidden behind your back. The curious axolotls swim toward you. They poke their adorable faces out of the water and stare at you. Then, you strike!

With lightning-fast movements, you bring the bucket from behind your back and slosh it into the water. The axolotls flee, but not quickly enough. You lift the bucket out of the water. Inside, a pink axolotl swims in circles, confused.

The axolotl looks up at you and seems sad. You weaken. Either you need to free it or capture another one so it will have a companion.

If you free the axolotl, turn to page 60.
If you capture a companion, turn to page 61.

You look at the solitary pink axolotl and smile. It's too cute to keep in captivity. It's not a cow or a chicken. It deserves to be free and wild.

You stand at the edge of the lake and tip the bucket. The axolotl jumps into the water. It swims in circles for a moment and then surfaces. It seems like it is smiling at you. You wave goodbye and it dives into the lake to be with its friends.

With a smile on your face and a warm, fuzzy feeling in your soul, you continue into the depths of the cave system.

Turn to page 65.

You realize it would be cruel to keep the pink axolotl in isolation, so you decide to capture a companion. This time, you want a golden one.

You stalk the lakeshore until you see a golden axolotl bobbing in the water in the distance. You set down the bucket holding the pink axolotl. You remove another bucket from your inventory and fill it with water. Then, you pick up both buckets and approach your prey.

When you arrive near the golden axolotl, you set down the used bucket and take the empty one close to the shore. You dip the bucket into the water and scoop the golden axolotl into the bucket.

As you raise the bucket from the water, you suddenly feel a massive impact from behind. You are shoved into the water. The bucket slips from your hands and sinks to the bottom of the lake, allowing the golden axolotl to go free.

You tread water as you cough to clear water from your lungs. Then, you turn around to see what hit you. You gasp when you see a spider jockey! It is a cave spider ridden by a skeleton with a bow. It quickly shoots an arrow at you, but misses.

You have no choice but to fight.

Turn the page.

As you climb out of the water, you pull your sword. The spider jockey shoots another arrow. This time, it hits you in the chest. You growl and rush toward the mob.

You ignore the skeleton rider and strike at the spider first. It doesn't take long before it poofs. Now, the skeleton is standing and shoots an arrow at you. You duck and bullrush the skeleton. You knock it to the ground. It tries to stand up, but you don't let it. You slash at it without mercy until it flashes red and disappears in a puff of smoke.

You are breathing hard. You walk back to the lakeshore and look into the water. You can just see your bucket at the bottom of the lake. You are about to jump in to retrieve it, when you hear a cacophony.

BRRrrrrr. Skittter. BRRrrrrr. Skittter. Crunch. Moan.

It sounds like an army of mobs is descending on your location. You don't want to run, but you probably should. Still, if you could defeat all the mobs coming your way, it would give you a massive boost of XP.

If you stand your ground and fight, turn to page 63.
If you grab the pink axolotl and run, turn to page 64.

Well, you think as a dozen skeletons, seven zombies, four spiders, and two creepers rush toward you, *that was the worst decision I've ever made.*

That battle is short and vicious.

You don't last long.

As you fall onto your side, you see the bucket holding the pink axolotl. Your final thought before you poof is of the cute little creature who will spend eternity trapped inside of a bucket.

You poof.

If you'd like to respawn to the prior page and make a different decision, turn to page 62.

If you want to go to the start of this book, turn to page 1.

You love the idea of gaining loads of experience points, but it sounds like over twenty mobs are coming your way. You would also like to get your sunken bucket back, but sometimes it's better just to accept the things you cannot change.

You sprint to the bucket containing the pink axolotl. You pick it up and put it into your inventory. Then, you head toward the exit of the lush cave and venture further down into the depths.

Turn to page 65.

You move along and soon enter a medium-width passage, averaging ten blocks wide. You follow it as it slowly tilts in a downward direction. As you walk, you place torches to mark your path and prevent hostile mobs from spawning.

After a few minutes, the passage opens into a wide, but not massive, cavern. On the far side of the cavern is a narrow lava fall, filling a small lava pond. Closer to where you stand, a waterfall tumbles down a stone wall into a wide creek, flowing slowly through the center of the cavern. You see an exit on the other side of the chamber.

As you walk toward the exit, you explore the chamber. You are happy when you find a deposit of copper ore. You make quick work of it, acquiring seventeen copper ore blocks.

As you are tucking the last block into your inventory, you notice a strange cloud drifting through the cave. You didn't think clouds could exist underground. You stare at the cloud for a moment and then realize you were correct. It is not a cloud; it's a swarm of bats!

Even though bats don't cause much damage, you find them horribly annoying since they don't have any drops, not even XP.

If you stay and kill the bats, turn to page 66.

If you ignore the bats and continue into the depths, turn to page 67.

You're kind of cruel, aren't you?

You wait for the defenseless bats to approach, and then you slash at them with your sword. You poof two of them right away. The remaining six bats squeak and fly away.

You pull your bow and shot the rest of the bats with arrows.

You feel powerful—for a moment. Then, you feel stupid. You just wasted six arrows on harmless, passive mobs.

You shake your head and berate yourself. At least you got some copper. You turn and walk to the exit of the cavern and continue exploring the cave.

Turn to page 67.

You pass through the chamber's exit and into a narrow passage. You travel without incident for nearly ten minutes, placing torches as you walk. You arrive at a dead end.

"This is so frustrating," you mutter, stomping your foot on the ground.

You stand at the edge of a precipice, a sheer cliff dropping into a dark abyss. You think you see a small lava pond in the depths, but without an elytra, it will take hours to build a staircase to get down there. You are about to turn back, when you notice something.

You crouch and cautiously approach the edge of the cliff. You peek over and see the top of a ladder! Someone has built a ladder leading down into the abyss.

If you climb down the ladder, turn to page 68.

If you are too afraid to climb down the ladder and decide to return home, turn to page 144.

You decide to go for it. Worst-case scenario, you plummet to your doom and respawn. Sure, you'll probably lose a lot of your loot, but you prefer adventure to certainty.

It is awkward climbing down the ladder. You descend slowly, placing torches in the cliff face to illuminate the path, checking to make sure the ladder doesn't suddenly end above an abyss.

When you've been climbing down for a couple minutes, you startle and nearly lose your grip when you see a sign affixed to the sheer wall next to the ladder. You place a torch beside it so it is easier to read:

"Great treasure awaits, but only for those who can avoid certain death."

You aren't sure whether to believe the sign or roll your eyes. Most likely it is just some player trying to prevent anyone else from discovering something super amazing at the bottom of the ladder. Still, you've heard of a monster who lurks at the bottom of caves. Maybe that is what the sign means by "certain death"? Maybe that is where this ladder ends?

If you heed the mysterious warning and return home, turn to page 144.

If you want to continue climbing down the ladder and search for the treasure, turn to page 69.

The ladder continues downward for quite some distance. Because you are descending so cautiously, you take nearly ten minutes to reach the bottom.

You step off the ladder onto level ground. You raise a torch to explore the area when you hear hurried footfalls. You grip your sword, readying for battle.

An unnatural shriek echoes through the cave. The footsteps are louder. This is it.

You spot an open doorway a few paces ahead just as a player, her eyes wide like she's seen a ghost, rushes through the same doorway toward you. She falls to her knees and looks up at you. She does not appear to be sane.

"Don't go in there!" she wails. "There's a monster. My friends. They all poofed!"

You shiver. This player is terrified, not merely scared. *Terrified.* There is something horrible down here.

"What was it?" you ask, shaking her shoulders. "What did you see?"

The player's lower lip trembles, like she's trying to form words. Instead, she jumps to her feet, shrieks again, and then climbs up the ladder as quickly as she can.

Maybe you should be satisfied with the copper ore and go home?

If you abandon the cave and return home, turn to page 144.

If you ignore the player's warning and proceed through the doorway, turn to page 111.

You wish you had a three-sided coin so you could flip it and decide which passage to take. As you look at the options, it seems to you that the entrance to the right-most passage is a block or two closer to where you are standing. You take this realization as an omen and enter the right passage.

The passage is narrow. As you walk, you place torches at intervals, to mark your path and to keep mobs from spawning. After about thirty paces, the passage widens. You see that the passage continues straight ahead as far as you can see. You also notice an opening to your left.

Transferring your torch to your off hand, you pull your diamond sword. You creep toward the opening, worried that something might be lurking inside. You press your body against the wall near the opening. You lean over and turn your head to see what is inside....

Turn the page.

Yeah, you were right—something is lurking inside. From where you stand, you can see three zombies and a chest!

BRRrrrr. BRRrrrr. BRRrrrr.

The zombies all notice you at the same moment. This could get ugly. Fortunately, you have options.

If you brick up the opening with cobblestone, turn to page 72.

If you stand and fight, turn to page 73.

If you toss a block of TNT into the room, turn to page 75.

You drop your torch and sword and pull a stack of cobblestone blocks from your inventory. With sweat dripping from your forehead, you place blocks as quickly as you can.

The zombies seem to understand your plan. They sprint—well, what zombies call a sprint—toward you. But you are faster. You've already got two rows of blocks in front of the opening.

The lead zombie takes a swipe at you, scratching your hand, but that is all. You put the third and final row of blows in front of the opening and seal it closed.

You are sad you won't get to see what was in the chest, but you want to explore the cave and find copper, not risk your life for a chest that might be empty.

Turn to page 77.

With an animalistic growl, you rush at the zombies. You make quick work of the first one, but the second one lands a surprisingly powerful blow against your head. You stagger back for a moment.

While you recover, the third zombie joins. They try to flank you, but you are too quick. You begin to spin like a top, holding the sword out, slashing both zombies with each completed rotation. Sure, they get in a few hits on you, but soon, they both poof.

You stop spinning and feel dizzy. As you struggle to stay upright, another zombie emerges from the entrance to the chamber!

You lunge at it. This zombie is wearing an iron helmet, so it takes an extra two slashes to dispose of it.

After you regain your breath, you approach the chest tucked in the corner of the room.

Turn the page.

You punch the chest open.

Inside, you find a loaf of bread, some spider string, three rotten flesh, and a wooden pickaxe.

"Lame," you mutter. Nevertheless, you grab the bread and spider string before slamming the chest shut.

You shake your head as you realize what a waste of time this was. You should have just bricked up the entrance and moved on.

Turn to page 77.

It might be loud and messy, but TNT almost always gets the job done.

As the zombies lurch toward you, you pull a TNT block and your flint and steel from your inventory. You ignite the block and toss it into the room. Then, you run!

A few seconds pass and then: *KA-BLAMmmmm*! The shock wave from the explosion knocks you to the floor of the passage.

When you recover, you hold up a torch and peer into the smoke-filled air. You wave your hand in front of your face, trying to get a better look.

A zombie lunges from the smoke and bashes a fist against your head. *BRRrrrr.*

Turn the page.

You fumble for your sword, as the zombie punches you again. Thankfully, you are wearing diamond armor and you aren't a noob. You don't panic.

Finally, you get a grip on our sword and slash at the zombie. It doesn't last long. After the zombie poofs, you cautiously enter the smokey air. You want to make sure all the zombies are gone. You don't want them sneaking up on you later.

When you arrive at the opening, you see a giant crater where the chamber used to be. In fact, the crater doesn't have a bottom. You look over the edge but see only darkness.

What could be down there?

You return to the passage and continue your exploration of the cave.

Turn the page.

You continue deeper into the cave. The passage you are in widens and narrows at random intervals, but always continues downward.

After a few minutes, you enter a large chamber. A massive lava lake illuminates most of the chamber so brightly that you don't need torches. Still, you continue to place torches at wider intervals to mark your path so you will be able to find your way out.

As you explore the chamber, looking for copper or a way to go further into the depths of the cave, you notice something astonishing: a nether portal!

It isn't operational, but it is complete. All you need to do is ignite it and you can travel to the Nether. Maybe you could find some ancient debris to help craft netherite? But, the reason you went questing today was to find copper ore. Still, traveling to the Nether is tempting.

If you ignore the nether portal and continue exploring, turn to page 101.

If you ignite the portal and go to the Nether, turn to page 78.

The Nether? Awesome!

You pull out your flint and steel. You approach the obsidian frame. You reach into the empty space and strike a spark. The nether portal roars to life, its center now resembling a gauzy purple sheet undulating in a gentle breeze.

You take a deep breath. You weren't really expecting to journey to the Nether today. You don't feel prepared. But, you won't stay long. You just plan to look around a bit and then return to exploring the cave.

After all, what could go wrong?

You take another deep breath and step into the portal.

Turn the page.

The heat. It's the first thing you notice when you step out of the portal. Then the lack of humidity hits you like a golem punch to the face. You've heard people say that they don't mind a "dry heat," but at that moment, you think they are crazy. If the Nether wasn't known to be dangerous, you'd strip off your armor and walk around in a t-shirt and pants. Unfortunately, that isn't an option.

You survey your surroundings.

Everywhere you look is netherrack. The only disruption to the uniform landscape is bright streams of lava flowing here and there. You've heard there are some pretty cool biomes in the Nether, but this clearly isn't one of them.

You note the location of the nether portal so you can get back to the Overworld. Then, you start exploring.

You don't see much of interest for the first couple of minutes. Then, you walk around an outcropping of netherrack and spot three zombified piglins milling about in the distance.

Turn the page.

You duck behind the outcropping while you think about your next move.

You try to recall what you know about zombified piglins. It isn't much. You know they are undead, neutral mobs. Unlike piglins, they don't barter. Basically, unless you want to harvest any potential drops, there is no point in attacking them. Still, it might be fun to get a closer look at them.

If you approach the zombified piglins, turn to page 82.

If you ignore the zombified piglins and continue exploring, turn to page 84.

If you return to the nether portal and exit the Nether, turn to page 81.

On second thought, what are you doing? The Nether is totally different than exploring a cave, and a lot more dangerous. You wave to the zombified piglins, who ignore you, before you return to the nether portal and resume your exploration of the cave.

You continue exploring the massive cavern and spot an opening about one hundred blocks away. As you walk toward it, you spot the telltale indications of copper ore.

"Yes!" you shout. Your voice echoes inside the massive chamber.

You pull your diamond pickaxe and, over the course of the next ten minutes, are able to mine almost one hundred copper ore blocks. Your copper roof dreams are coming true.

After you finish mining, you eat some roasted beef and a couple of chicken legs. Then, you turn toward the opening leading further into the depths.

Turn to page 102.

You walk slowly and casually toward the zombified piglins. They eye you with suspicion and close ranks, but do not make any hostile move toward you. At least what you heard about them being neutral is true.

You are feeling brave, so you get within a step of one of the mobs. You smile at it, hoping for a positive response. Instead, it glowers at you and then turns its back to you.

Rude!

You decide zombified piglins are boring. If you had more time, you might make them poof and harvest their drops, but you're not in the mood.

If you continue exploring the Nether, turn to page 83.

If you return to the nether portal and exit the Nether, turn to page 81.

You scowl at the boring mobs and turn to walk away. Your toe catches on a rock and you fall. This wouldn't be so bad if you were simply embarrassed. Unfortunately, you fall into one of the zombified piglins!

The creature growls at you and attacks. He is joined by his two friends. You are surrounded.

You take minor damage before you can get to your feet and pull your diamond sword. The trio closes on you. You slash at one of them. It moans and backs away. You dash through the small opening created by his absence. Now, you can face all three at once.

The battle doesn't take long. You win an easy victory, but still lost nearly a third of your health. You eat some food to restore it.

Maybe coming to the Nether wasn't such a good idea?

If you continue exploring the Nether, turn to page 84.

If you return to the nether portal and exit the Nether, turn to page 100.

You continue wandering through the nether wastes biome for a few more minutes. It is *so boring*. Netherrack and lava as far as the eye can see.

Wait a minute? What's that up ahead?

You squint your eyes and see a large red fungus in the distance. You gasp at the realization that you must be approaching the edge of a crimson forest biome. You've heard about that biome. It sounds pretty cool. You run toward it.

When you arrive at the edge of the biome two minutes later, you marvel at how strange it is. The ground is covered almost entirely with red fungus. There are just hints of netherrack peeking through here and there. In the distance, you see a herd of hoglins. You've heard that these boar-like hostile mobs are a good source of food, but you decide today is not the day to go hunting.

Turn the page.

You enter the biome and harvest some of the fungus and a few weeping vines. This doesn't take long, and soon you are ready to continue exploring. When you walk around the trunk of a huge crimson fungus, you see something so incredible that you gasp.

It is a dwelling, obviously constructed by a player. It isn't very large, about twenty blocks long and ten blocks wide. The roof is about four blocks high. There is a single door and two windows. You wonder if anyone is home.

If you approach the dwelling, turn to page 87.

If you continue exploring, turn to page 86.

If you return to the portal and exit the Nether, turn to page 100.

You don't feel like talking to any other players. Even if the dwelling is empty, it isn't cool to trespass on other players' property. You decide to continue exploring.

You walk through the crimson forest biome for another few minutes. As you do, you are careful to avoid hoglins and piglins. If you had golden armor, you might try bartering with the piglins. But, with diamond armor, you'd have a fight on your hands. You think you'd be victorious, but you don't want to fight if you don't have to.

You look ahead and see a new biome: a soul sand valley.

Turn to page 93.

You take cautious footsteps toward the small house, made mostly of red fungus blocks and cobblestone. The latter must have been brought from the Overworld.

When you get to the house, you knock on the door. No answer. You knock harder. Again, no response. You assume the owner of the dwelling is not home.

You walk to one of the windows and peek inside. It is sparsely furnished. You see a brewing stand and a chest. There is also an armor stand with a suit of gold armor. You wonder what might be inside the chest.

If you enter the dwelling and search the chest, turn to page 89.

If you ignore the dwelling and continue exploring, turn to page 88.

If you return to the portal and exit the Nether, turn to page 100.

The interior of the dwelling looks interesting. There are even some cool items to loot. But, it isn't cool to trespass on other players' property. You wouldn't want someone doing that to your home base. You decide to continue exploring.

You walk through the crimson forest biome for another few minutes. As you do, you are careful to avoid hoglins and piglins. If you had golden armor, you might try bartering with the piglins. But, with diamond armor, you'd have a fight on your hands. You think you'd be victorious, but you don't want to fight if you don't have to.

You look ahead and see a new biome: a soul sand valley.

Turn to page 93.

You punch open the door and enter the dwelling. You glance over your shoulder to make sure no one is watching you and then you make a beeline to the chest. You punch it open.

Whoa!

The chest is filled with many items, including gold ingots, blaze rods, warped fungus, and—stacks of netherite ingots! There are so many, you don't think the player will miss a few. I mean, what is the harm in taken a dozen ingots from someone who has hundreds?

If you steal the ingots, turn to page 90.

If you close the chest and leave the dwelling and continue exploring, turn to page 92.

If you close the chest and decide to leave the Nether, turn to page 99.

You rub your hands together like a greedy villager. Sure, you know stealing is wrong, but this will save you tons of time hunting for ancient debris. Besides, whoever lives here clearly knows how to acquire netherite ingots with ease.

You grab twelve ingots and stuff them into your inventory. You close the lid to the chest. You are about to turn and leave the dwelling when your body erupts with pain.

You turn and see a player, clad head-to-toe in netherite armor, blocking the doorway.

"You threw a harming potion at me, didn't you?" you say. "I was just looking around."

The player laughs. "Yeah, right," she says. "I always throw splash potions at thieves!"

You realize she saw what you did. There is no point in denying it.

"So what now?" you ask.

"Now, you poof," she says. She stands still for a moment, but then glares malevolently at you and charges.

You raise your diamond sword to defend yourself. You land a few strikes, but you are no match for this player. Not only are her armor and weapons better than yours, but her skills as a warrior make you look like a noob.

The last thing you see before you poof is her looking down at you, sneering.

If you'd like to respawn on the prior page and make a different decision, turn to page 89.

If you'd like to start this adventure at the beginning, turn to page 1.

As tempting as it is to steal the netherite, along with some of the other items in the chest, you don't do it. You would hate it if someone invaded your house and stole your hard-earned loot. You may not be the most noble player to ever spawn, but you aren't a thief or a griefer.

You close the lid to the chest and walk out the front door, closing it behind you. As you stand in front of the dwelling, deciding your next move, you suddenly feel as though you are being watched. It is an uncomfortable feeling to be sure. You scan the surrounding area, trying to find the source of your discomfort, but you see nothing.

You shiver and turn away from the dwelling to continue your explorations.

You walk through the crimson forest biome for another few minutes. As you do, you are careful to avoid hoglins and piglins. If you had golden armor, you might try bartering with the piglins. But, with diamond armor, you'd have a fight on your hands. You think you'd be victorious, but you don't want to fight if you don't have to.

You look ahead and see a new biome: a soul sand valley.

Turn the page.

You stare in wonder at this bone-dry biome. Beyond some blocks of gravel separating the crimson forest from this new biome, a carpet of soul sand and soul soil spreads before you. Scattered throughout the biome, you spot telltale blue flames: soul fire. You aren't sure why, but this biome gives you the creeps.

You see movement in the distance and realize it is a strider. It is the first one you've seen. For a moment, you think about running after it and trying to ride it. But that could be dangerous. Instead, you enter the biome, walking in a direction taking you away from the strider.

Banks of fog drift by. The bizarre, disembodied sound of ... *something* fills the air. Is it the sound of souls? Is that why this is known as "soul" sand? And "soul" fire? You shiver and push the thoughts from your mind.

In the distance, you notice one area with gigantic basalt columns. Some distance to the right of the columns you see what appears to be a massive, irregular structure sticking out of the ground. Both locations seem interesting.

If you explore the irregular structure, turn to page 94.

If you explore the basalt columns, turn to page 95.

If you decide to stop exploring and return to the nether portal to leave the Nether, turn to page 100.

As you get closer to the strange structure, you have an uneasy feeling. You realize with a shudder that you aren't looking at a structure, but ancient bones. It's the fossilized rib cage of a massive creature!

You approach the rib cage and rub your hand against it. It is rough and cold to the touch. *What sort of creature could drop something so huge when it poofed?* You are thankful that you did not live at the same time as something so massive. *It must have been dangerous.*

You decide to harvest some of the fossil as a souvenir. You remove your pickaxe and mine two large bone blocks from the fossil and put them in your inventory. You already know the perfect place to display them at your base.

You turn and look toward the basalt columns. To your surprise, they've vanished! There is nothing there now but soul sand and soul fire. You have no idea how such an enormous natural creation could have vanished in a few brief minutes.

Was it possible that descendants of the massive creatures who left the fossil still remain, lurking under the sand? Did they undermine the basalt column?

Whatever happened, you don't like it. You decide that now is not the time to explore the Nether. You flee from the soul sand valley.

Turn to page 100.

When you arrive at the base of the black columns, you marvel at them. There are a few dozen at least, some of which reach to the roof of the Nether. You wonder at the geologic forces that could have created such magnificent structures.

You pull out your pickaxe and harvest a few basalt blocks. You might use them as a plinth for the statue you plan to build of yourself and display in your front yard. Or maybe you'll just use them as items of visual interest in the walls of your base. Either way, it will look cool.

You are about to explore the strange, irregular structure when you notice something in the distance. You walk toward it and soon realize that it is an inactive nether portal! All you need to do is ignite it and you'll be back in the Overworld. Of course, you have no idea where you might end up.

If you enter the new nether portal, turn to page 96.

If you turn around and explore the irregular structure, turn to page 94.

If you return to the original nether portal to return to the cave in the Overworld, turn to page 100.

You only live once, right? Well, actually, you respawn indefinitely, so maybe that saying doesn't have much bearing on your decision.

Anyway, you pull out your flint and steel and ignite the mysterious nether portal. You hope you end up somewhere near your house or, if not there, then somewhere cool. You take a deep breath and step into the portal.

The world turns purple and swirls around you for a few seconds and then ... you find yourself inside a small room, illuminated by torches. The nether portal is in the center of the floor. You notice a wooden door a few paces away.

If you open the door, turn to page 98.

If you reenter the nether portal and return to the Nether, turn to page 97.

"This room is lame," you mutter.

You have no idea what is on the other side of the door and don't want to find out. You reenter the nether portal.

When you materialize in the Nether, you deactivate the portal and trudge back to the original portal you used to enter the Nether the first time. You jump in and find yourself back in the cave.

Turn to page 102.

As a precaution, you deactivate the nether portal. Then, you cautiously approach the door and open it slowly.

On the other side, you see a narrow passage lined with torches. It looks like you are underground and that someone has carved the passage from solid rock.

You proceed down the tunnel. After twenty paces, you come to on opening. You step through it and find yourself inside a cavern in a cave.

It might even be the same cave you were in earlier, just some other part of it. You shrug. Since you are in a cave, you decide to keep exploring. If you get tired, you'll sleep underground. Eventually, you'll come to the surface and figure out where you are.

Turn to page 49.

As tempting as it is to steal the netherite, along with some of the other items in the chest, you don't do it. You would hate it if someone invaded your house and stole your hard-earned loot. You may not be the most noble player to ever spawn, but you aren't a thief or a griefer.

You close the lid to the chest and walk out the front door, closing it behind you. As you stand in front of the dwelling, deciding your next move, you suddenly feel as though you are being watched. It is an uncomfortable feeling, to be sure. You scan the surrounding area, trying to find the source of your discomfort, but you see nothing.

You shiver and then head back to the nether portal. It was fun exploring the Nether for a while, but you realize you are out of your element. Besides, you like exploring caves.

When you arrive at the nether portal safely, you heave a sigh of relief and then step into the purple doorway. You materialize back inside the cave.

Turn to page 102.

You've had enough of the Nether. You return quickly and quietly to the nether portal, avoiding all contact with mobs. You step through the portal and return to the cave.

You continue exploring the massive cavern and spot an opening about one hundred blocks away. As you walk toward it, you spot the telltale indications of copper ore.

"Yes!" you shout. Your voice echoes inside the massive chamber.

You pull your diamond pickaxe and, over the course of the next ten minutes, are able to mine almost one hundred copper ore blocks. Your copper roof dreams are coming true.

After you finish mining, you eat some roasted beef and a couple of chicken legs. Then, you turn toward the opening leading further into the depths.

Turn to page 102.

As cool as it would be to explore the Nether, it is also a bit sketchy. You've been to the Nether once before and nearly poofed. Now that you know the portal is here, you can return later, if you want.

You continue exploring the massive cavern and spot an opening about one hundred blocks away. As you walk toward it, you see the telltale indications of copper ore in the ground.

"Yes!" you shout. Your voice echoes inside the massive chamber.

You pull your diamond pickaxe and, over the course of the next ten minutes, are able to mine almost one hundred copper ore blocks. Your copper roof dreams are coming true.

After you finish mining, you eat some roasted beef and a couple of chicken legs. Then, you turn toward the opening leading further into the depths.

Turn the page.

You wind through a featureless corridor inside the cave for what seems like hours, even though it is probably only ten minutes. Oddly, there are no side passages and no signs of ore. You are ready to give up and start mining holes into the walls of the passage when you see something glint up ahead, reflecting your torchlight.

You raise your torch higher into the air and squint your eyes, but you can't tell what is so shiny. Diamonds? Gold?

You switch your torch to your off-hand and grip your diamond sword tightly in your dominant hand. You walk forward, slowly, until you see what was shining. It is the blade of a diamond sword embedded into the ground.

The blade is vertical, like a post. Lashed to the hilt with leather straps is a birch wood sign that reads:

"Great treasure awaits, but only for those who can avoid certain death."

Awaits where? you think. You're at the dead end of a passage.

You spin around, trying to figure out where this so-called treasure is allegedly awaiting. And then, you look down and realize you are standing on a trap door.

"Oh, no!" you yelp. You are about to jump away when the trap door snaps open and you fall into a dark abyss.

Turn the page.

You scream as you plummet into utter darkness. You can't see anything. You don't know if you are going to hit the ground in a second, a minute, or never.

You've always heard there was a void surrounding the End. Could it be possible that somehow that trap door was a mysterious opening to the void?

Your mind races. You try to think of anything in your inventory that could help you. Sadly, you have never been to the End, so you don't have an elytra. You flick through everything in your inventory and realize there is nothing you can do. You will soon poof.

If you give up and accept your fate, turn to page 104.

If you keep thinking of some way to survive, turn to page 105.

It is sad that it is going to end like this. All you had to do was spot that trap door. If only you had been paying attention.

"Stupid," you mutter.

Another second passes and then ...

... you slam into the ground and ...

... you poof.

If you'd like to respawn on the prior page and make a different decision, turn to page 103.

If you want to start a new adventure, turn to page 1.

"Think, fool," you scream. "Think!"

You bang your fists against your head. Maybe you can knock an idea loose?

You swear you feel a *thunk* inside your brain. Suddenly, you have a moment of clarity.

A water bucket! Of course.

You yank a bucket full of water from your inventory and hold it underneath your feet. If you are lucky, the water bucket will limit your fall damage. You just hope you land feet first. Otherwise, things are going to get ugly.

You feel the wind rushing by and then *SPLASH!*

You slam into the ground, landing inside your water bucket. You are still alive.

"Yes!" you yell as you ignite a torch.

You survey your surroundings and discover you are in a small room with no exits other than the immense column of space above your head and a small wooden door in front of you. Unless you want to poof because of starvation, you have to open the door. It's your only choice.

You switch the torch to your off hand and pull a sword. You move forward confidently and punch open the door.

Turn the page.

Beyond the door is a large, but not massive, cavern. A narrow stream of lava provides enough light to see that the cavern is maybe fifty blocks in any direction from its center point. You can't be sure, but you get the sense that this cavern was carved out of stone rather than generated naturally.

You enter the cavern farther. Other than the door through which you just came, the only other way out of the cavern is an irregular opening all the way on the other side, about fifty blocks away. You heave a sigh and start walking. If you want to get back to the surface, you need to find a way out. You could, of course, build a staircase, but you'd rather not have to do so much work.

About a minute later, you are about to step through the opening when an enderman steps through it. As luck would have it, you are so surprised that you stare *directly* into his eyes.

The enderman screeches with rage and teleports directly in front of you. You've got a fight on your hands.

If you stand your ground and fight, turn to page 107.
If you try to find a way to escape, turn to page 110.

Even though you find endermen to be the most terrifying of all mobs, you stand and fight. When you were a noob, you would have run for your life.

The enderman screeches and slams into you, causing over three hearts of damage. That hurt. You growl and slash at the enderman with your diamond sword. The enderman shrieks. You must have landed a critical hit!

The enderman teleports away. You crouch against the wall. He won't be able to sneak up on you from behind.

Nearly thirty seconds pass. Maybe the enderman decided to leave you alone?

Screech!

The enderman seems to come out of nowhere. He smacks you on the side of your head.

"Oof," you grunt as you stumble to the side. Your health bar is dropping. You are beginning to think maybe you should have tried to escape earlier.

You charge away from the enderman, hoping you can somehow escape. He teleports in front of you and attacks. You slash at him with your sword. You land a few blows, and the enderman begins to flash red.

"Yes!" you shout. But then, a bolt of fear passes through you when you notice you are flashing red too!

If you take one final swipe at the enderman, turn to page 108.

If you drink a healing potion, turn to page 109.

You grit your teeth. You know you are in a life-or-poof situation. You hold your ground and bring your sword back. The enderman, flashing between black and red so fast that he almost appears to be purple, screeches and lunges for you.

You drop to one knee and slash your sword with all your might.

The enderman poofs! You escape further injury.

You slump to the ground, breathing hard. You eat some bread and drink a healing potion. That was close.

After you recover sufficiently, you stand and nod proudly. That was a fine battle. You congratulate yourself for surviving. But now, it's time to find the treasure promised by the mysterious sign.

Turn to page 111.

You know you don't stand a chance unless you can get some of your health back. If the enderman lands even a glancing blow, it's over for you.

You back away quickly from the enderman. You fumble in your inventory and find a healing potion. You put the stopper of the bottle between your teeth and pull it out.

But, just before the salubrious nectar can pass through your lips, the enderman teleports in front of you and bashes your head between its two tiny fists.

You poof.

If you want to respawn on the prior page and make a different decision, turn to page 107.

If you want to start this adventure at the beginning, turn to page 1.

Even though you have no idea where you are, you run. The enderman shrieks and follows. You run back toward the tiny room where you landed inside your bucket of water.

No, you think, *that's a dead end.*

You are about to turn in a new direction when you suddenly remember something. You grin like a fox. *This is going to be easy.*

You race toward the small room, the enderman teleporting directly behind you. He swipes at you a few times, doing moderate amounts of damage. If your plan works, you could be down to a single heart and it wouldn't matter.

Finally, you make it to the room. You spin on your foot and place cobblestone blocks in the air inside the doorway so that the entire entrance is blocked except for the lowest two block levels.

The enderman howls with rage. He's three blocks tall, so he can't get to you. You laugh like a maniac as you slash at the angry enderman's legs. You can damage him, but he can't damage you.

It doesn't take long. The enderman poofs. You grab the ender pearl he dropped.

You heave a thankful sigh. You pull out your pickaxe and remove the cobblestone barrier. You reenter the larger carven and head toward the entrance on the opposite side. It's time to find the treasure the sign promised you.

Turn to page 111.

You step through the doorway and enter a massive cavern. But it doesn't look at all like a part of the cave. It appears to be the ruins of an ancient city!

Directly in front of you is a covered walkway. Deepslate pillars line both sides of the walkway. Across the tops of the pillars is a thick crossbeam, also made of deepslate. The entire walkway cover resembles a long, thin rib cage of a creature that has thirty pairs of ribs.

Everywhere, you see the flicker of candles and the glow of soul lanterns. It is bright enough that you no longer need your torch. You extinguish it and put it back into your inventory. You marvel at the candles and lanterns. You wonder who ignited them—and when? Are these ruins inhibited, or have the candles and lanterns burned for centuries alone, waiting for someone to arrive?

To your left and right, you see stairways. Each leads to a walkway about four blocks above the floor where you now stand. Like the covered walkway, the raised paths appear to lead to the same location: a massive imposing stone edifice at the other end of the cavern.

"The treasure must be in there," you mutter.

The edifice is over two hundred blocks away. Your only task is to get there. So, how do you do it?

If you use the raised path to the right, turn to page 112.

If you use the raised path to the left, turn to page 116.

If you use the covered walkway, turn to page 122.

You grip your diamond sword and climb the stone stairs. When you get to the pathway itself, you are startled to find that it is made of light gray wool.

"Bizarre," you mumble.

You have no idea why anyone would craft a pathway with such material. You begin to walk along the pathway and soon notice that your footsteps are nearly silent. You could probably sneak up on anything if you could walk on wool the entire time.

As you move along the path, you glance down at the lower floor and notice something growing or spreading on the stone below.

It is mostly black and dark blue, with flecks of lighter blue and green. Here and there, some of the blocks appear to have leaves or maybe tendrils growing out of them, swaying gently as though there were a breeze in the cavern.

You've heard rumors that strange things lurk in the deepest parts of caves, but you've never heard any eyewitness accounts. Just gossip and hearsay.

Some players have told you that the only players who return from the Deep Dark have gone insane, raving about shrieking creatures and an unkillable, soul-stealing golem. You never believed these ridiculous stories.

However, now that you are deep inside a cave, you are feeling as though maybe you should have thought through this expedition a bit more. Still, you've gone nearly halfway to the massive edifice without incident.

Perhaps the rumors you've heard were started to keep other players away from the treasure the sign promised?

As you take your next step, you notice a stone balcony attached to the wool path. On top of the balcony, a chest rests.

If you open the chest, turn to page 114.

If you ignore the chest and continue walking, turn to page 115.

The number one rule of life, as far as you're concerned, is: if you see a stray chest, you loot it. You stand in front of the chest and punch it open.

The chest opens with a loud *creeeaaak!*

Before you can check its contents, one of the strange blocks with the tentacles growing out of it vibrates and then makes a peculiar noise: *sculk*. It is almost as though the noise from the chest caused the block to react.

SHRIEK!

You duck as a bone curdling shriek rises from another nearby block. You pull your sword and get ready for an attack by some sort of shriek monster. A massive, two-headed enderman maybe?

After a minute without an attack, you stand up and survey the area. You notice that your vision is pulsing in and out of darkness. Did the shriek cause that? Is it some sort of debuff to make your exploration more difficult?

"Just great," you groan. You pull a torch to use when your vision darkens. You hope this is a temporary debuff.

You look inside the chest and groan again. The chest is empty. You can't help but think if you didn't open the chest, none of the sculking and shrieking and debuffing would have happened.

You shake your head and sigh. You continue toward the edifice.

Turn to page 126.

You think seriously about opening the chest, but then you decide against it. You assume that if there is truly a great treasure hidden somewhere in this ancient city, it won't be sitting in a chest in plain sight. You decide to continue exploring. You'll open the chest on your way out.

You walk along the quiet, wool-covered pathway for a few more steps until you come to a three-block portion of the path made of deepslate. You inspect the area for traps and, once satisfied there are none, you stride forward on the stone.

Your diamond boots make a surprisingly loud clicking sound on the stone.

SHRIEK!

You duck as a bone-curdling shriek rises from a block on the floor below the raised pathway. You pull your sword and get ready for an attack by some sort of shriek monster. A massive, two-headed enderman maybe?

After a minute passes without any attack, you stand up and survey the area. You notice that your vision is pulsing in and out of darkness. Did the shriek cause that? Is it some sort of debuff to make your exploration more difficult?

"Just great," you groan.

You are back on wool now. You pull a torch to use when your vision darkens. You hope this is a temporary debuff.

You sigh and move toward the massive edifice.

Turn to page 126.

You grip your diamond sword and climb the stone stairs.

When you get to the pathway itself, you are startled to find that it is made of light gray wool. You have no idea why anyone would use wool to construct a pathway, but there it is. You begin to walk along the pathway and soon notice that your footsteps are nearly silent. You could probably sneak up on anything if you could walk on wool the entire time.

As you move along the path, you glance down at the lower floor and notice something growing or spreading on the stone below. It is mostly black and dark blue, with flecks of lighter blue and green. Here and there, some of the blocks appear to have leaves or maybe tendrils growing out of them, swaying gently as though there were a breeze in the cavern.

You've heard rumors that strange things lurk in the deepest parts of caves, but you've never heard any details. Some players have told you that the only players who return have gone insane, raving about shrieking creatures and an unkillable, soul-stealing golem.

You never believed these ridiculous stories.

However, now that you are deep inside a cave, you are feeling as though maybe you should have thought through this expedition a bit more. Still, you've gone nearly halfway to the massive edifice without incident.

Perhaps the rumors were started to keep other players away from the treasure the sign promised?

You are about halfway along the pathway when you notice a small stone room attached to the path. The room is sealed by a wooden door. The room itself is three blocks in all directions, a perfect cube.

You wonder what is inside.

What do you do?

If you open the door to the room, turn to page 118.

If you ignore the room and continue along the path, turn to page 120.

When you open the door and look inside, you immediately feel uncomfortable. On the opposite side of the room, you see what appears to be a small altar. Two groups of three candles are burning on either side of the altar. A skull harvested from a skeleton rests in the middle of the altar.

You take a step inside.

Behind the altar, there is a small window, more of a slit, really. You lean forward and peek through the slit. You have a clear view of the covered walkway.

"Interesting," you mumble. "I wonder who used this room?"

You lean back and look at the skull. *Cool*, you think, *I could use this to decorate my base.* You reach out and grab the skull. As you pick it up, it scrapes against the stone altar. Barely a second passes when you hear a peculiar noise: *sculk*. It is almost as though the *sculk* is a response to the movement of the skull or maybe the scraping noise.

SHRIEK!

You duck as a bone-curdling shriek rises from something close to the room. You pull your sword and get ready for an attack by some sort of shriek monster. Part ravager, part enderman, maybe?

After a minute without an attack, you stand up and exit the room, tucking the skull into your inventory. You notice that your vision is pulsing in and out of darkness. Did the shriek cause that? Is it some sort of debuff to make your exploration more difficult?

"Just great," you groan.

You pull a torch to help you see better each time your vision darkens. You really hope this on-and-off darkness is a temporary debuff.

You shake your head and continue along the wool path toward the massive edifice.

Turn to page 126.

You think seriously about entering the room, but are worried an enemy might be inside. On the other hand, you've been exploring for some time now, and you haven't encountered, seen, or even heard any mobs or players. You assume you are alone.

Besides, if there is truly a great treasure hidden somewhere in this ancient city, it won't be inside a tiny room. You decide to continue exploring. You'll check the room on your way out.

As you walk along the quiet, wool-covered pathway, you stare down at the covered walkway in the room's center. You wonder if anything cool is hidden under the cover. As your mind drifts to what might be elsewhere, you somehow take a misstep and stumble. As you fall to the ground, your diamond sword clanks against the low stone walls surrounding the pathway.

SHRIEK!

You duck as a bone-curdling shriek rises from a block on the floor below the raised pathway. You ready yourself for an attack by some sort of shriek monster. A wither with three enderman heads maybe?

After a minute without any attack, you stand up and survey the area. You notice that your vision is pulsing in and out of darkness. Did the shriek cause that? Is it some sort of debuff to make your exploration more difficult?

"Just great," you groan.

You pull a torch to help you see better each time your vision darkens. You really hope this on-and-off darkness is a temporary debuff.

You shake your head and continue along the wool path toward the massive edifice.

Turn to page 126.

As you enter the covered path, you see that you are walking on a wide path made of deepslate. You wonder if deepslate is as common at the bottom of caves as cobblestone is on the surface.

As you continue walking, you realize there are candles everywhere. There are niches carved into each of the columns in which rest anywhere from two to four candles. It seems silly or wasteful to have so many candles burning in an abandoned city. You punch several groups of candles and add them to your inventory. They will look cool at your base.

As you walk, you glance at the floor at the sides of the pathway nearest the columns. You notice something growing or spreading on the stone, though it seems to stop at the border of the path. Whatever it is, it is mostly black and dark blue, with flecks of lighter blue and green. Here and there, some of the blocks appear to have leaves or maybe tendrils growing out of them, swaying gently as though there were a breeze in the cavern.

You've heard rumors that strange things lurk in the deepest parts of caves, but you've heard no specific details. Some players have told you that the only players to return have gone insane, raving about shrieking creatures and an unkillable, soul-stealing golem.

You never believed these ridiculous stories.

However, now that you are deep inside a cave, you are feeling as though maybe you should have thought through this expedition a bit more. Still, you've gone nearly halfway to the massive edifice without incident. Perhaps the rumors were started to keep other players away from the treasure the sign promised?

You shake your head to stop thinking about such things and continue walking toward the edifice.

Turn to page 124.

As you continue along the path, you notice the floor bordering the path seems to be getting thicker with the strange, spreading substance. You wonder what it is and how it grows. If it is a plant-like organism, you wonder what it uses for nutrition. If it is more like an animal, what does it eat?

You shiver and move forward, ever closer to the massive edifice. You look up at the edifice, trying to make out details of what lies ahead. But then, something closer to you catches your eye.

At the edge of the path is a bizarre block. The solid portion of the block is half as tall as a normal block. It has the same colorations as the strange substance spreading on the floor, except the center of it seems to be swirling, like it's alive. On each corner of the block, there is a single thin, white eruption. They resemble teeth or horns.

Even though you know you shouldn't do what you do next, you reach out with your diamond sword and poke the strange block.

SHRIEK!

You stumble back from the block. You drop your sword and clasp your hands over your ears, trying to protect them from the piercing sound. Finally, the shrieking stops and you lower your hands.

What was that about? Was that a defense mechanism, or a signal?

You pick up your sword to prepare for anything. You notice that your vision is pulsing in and out of darkness. Did the shriek cause that? Is it some sort of debuff to make your exploration more difficult?

"Just great," you groan.

You ignite a torch and hold it in your off hand. You may need it during the periods of darkness. You hope the debuff is only temporary.

You move forward toward the edifice.

Turn to page 126.

You are now standing directly in front of the edifice. You gaze up at it in awe.

The thick, stone edifice rises several dozen blocks high. A one-block high opening in the front—about five blocks above the ground—stretches horizontally for twenty blocks and is filled with the blue flicker of soul fire.

You wonder about the soul lanterns and soul fire. Could the residents of this ancient city have worshiped souls? Or, maybe, they worshiped a creature who *fed* on souls? You shake your head.

"I'm not writing a horror novel," you mutter. "Just find the treasure."

But maybe this *is* a horror story.

You glance to the side and see dozens of drops floating near the front of the edifice. They aren't mobs drops either. They are the drops of players who have poofed. You approach the loot. You notice an inordinate amount of snowballs among the weapons and food.

"Weird," you mumble as you walk through the drop piles and add the loot to your inventory. You glance around the room. What could have killed those players? More importantly, when did they poof?

As you contemplate those questions, you look back at the front of the edifice and the most obvious part of it: the massive door in its center. You assume the treasure is behind that door. You move closer. The door itself is made out of ... well, you aren't sure. It doesn't look like any material you've ever seen. It is dark in color, but it isn't obsidian, or basalt, or netherite.

Whatever it is, it is massive. The door is eight blocks high and five blocks wide. You assume it is at least as thick as the wall. It must be unbelievably strong.

To the side of the door, you see an iron lever. It must open the door. You've come this far, the treasure awaits. But, what about those drop piles? What happened to those players? Maybe it's time to turn back?

It is time to answer the only question that matters. Do you pull the lever?

If you pull the lever, turn to page 128.

If you are too scared and decide to abandon your quest and return home, turn to page 146.

You take a deep breath and pull the lever. It slides easily from its position pointing up to pointing down.

Nothing happens for nearly two seconds, and you begin to panic.

Did I just alert a monster to my presence?

Did the lever summon an evil player or hostile mob to attack me?

Your fears seem to be unfounded, however, as the massive door begins to slide *into* the wall. The mechanic of a door disappearing into a wall is startling enough, but what truly amazes you to the point of nearly causing a freak out is that the door moves *without any sound*. Not a creak. Not a pop. Not a scrape. Perfect silence. In fact, if you couldn't see the door moving, you wouldn't know it was happening.

Speaking of seeing, you haven't noticed a pulse of darkness in a few seconds. It seems as though the debuff has expired. But when you see what is behind the door, you keep your torch out.

Once the door is open, you see a large, dark space. The first few blocks of the interior are just barely visible, illuminated by the soul lanterns on the pillars behind where you are standing. You take a cautious step forward and raise your torch.

The floor is a combination of the bizarre black and blue, creeping substance and deepslate. Given your limited experience with the unknown substance, you plan to keep to the deepslate.

You step inside and notice two levers on the interior wall of the room. One is on the right side of the opening. One is on the left.

Do you want to pull a lever, or ignore them for now and move forward?

If you pull the lever on the left, turn to page 130.

If you pull the lever on the right, turn to page 134.

If you ignore the levers and proceed to investigate the room, turn to page 132.

You are sure the lever will do something. Maybe it will reveal the treasure. You smile at the thought.

You reach out and pull the lever to the left of the door.

Ziiip!

The massive door springs from inside the wall and slams shut with a loud crash! You are sealed inside the dark room.

Oh, no, you think as you flick the lever back up, trying to reopen the door.

But it won't budge.

Am I actually sealed inside this room?!?

You are starting to panic. How are you going to get out of here? Wait a minute—

The other lever!

You hold your torch up and fumble toward the other side of the door. But, before you can get there, something rises from the ground, blocking your way.

Under the torch light, you can't see all the details, but it is a massive beast. Its skin is similar to the spreading substance. It's like the creature is made of the substance or, at least, has colored itself that way to hide among the substance. Like a massive chameleon.

You grip your diamond sword tightly. You have no choice but to stand and face the beast. You slash at its legs. The beast howls and smashes you with its fist.

The impact is tremendous. You are knocked off your feet. All but one of your hearts has vanished.

"No," you croak. "I'm so close to the treasure."

The beast does not give any indication that it can understand you. As it stalks toward you, you notice something on—or *in*?—its chest: the shape of souls. Is it just elaborate camouflage or something more sinister? You'll never know the answer because the beast is now directly in front of you. It growls, lifts its massive foot off the ground, and stomps on you.

You poof.

If you would like to respawn on the prior page and made a different decision, turn to page 128.

If you would like to start this adventure at the beginning, turn to page 1.

You assume at least one of the levers closes the door. You have no idea what the other lever might do, so you leave them alone.

You creep forward into the room, taking just two steps before you hear a *click* from beneath your feet. You swallow hard and look down. Oops. You just stepped on a pressure plate! As you prepare for the inevitable explosion and poofing, you notice a dozen soul lanterns suddenly illuminate along the wall of the room. That must have been what the pressure plate was for: to turn on the lanterns.

You blink your eyes a couple times to get used to the light. The room is empty except for a massive wooden chest, at least ten times larger than a typical chest. *The treasure!* You grin and rub your hands together.

You approach the chest. It is so tall, you aren't sure you'll be able to see inside of it from where you are standing. You look around and notice a staircase leading to a platform alongside the chest.

You climb the stairs which are carpeted with light gray wool. The sound of your footsteps is muffled, almost entirely silent. When you are on the platform, you see a rope tied to the lid of the chest. You reach out and pull the chest open.

Creeeaaak.

SHRIEK!

Not again. You glance around the room to make sure nothing is coming after you. When nothing happens after ten seconds, you assume you are safe. Now, you can see what is inside the chest.

You lean over the chest, extending your torch to see what is inside. At first, you can't quite tell what it is. It looks like a jumble of items. Once your brain can account for the strange shadows being cast by your torch, you gasp. It is an armor stand with a set of armor. Only, it is not the size of normal armor. It is several times larger.

Looks like that would fit an iron golem, you think. *Or maybe something even larger.*

The armor looks like it is made with gold, diamonds, and emeralds. It must be worth a fortune. When you understand what you're looking at, you break into a chuckle. Not only will it be cool to display this armor at your base, but you will be the richest player in the history of the Overworld.

You are about to loot the chest, when you feel rumbling. You turn and see something rising out of the ground!

Turn to page 136.

You are sure the lever will do something. Maybe it will reveal the treasure. You smile at the thought. You reach out and pull the lever. A second passes and then a dozen soul lanterns on the wall of the chamber illuminate.

You blink your eyes a couple of times to get used to the light. The room is empty except for a massive wooden chest, at least ten times larger than a typical chest. *The treasure!* You grin and rub your hands together.

You approach the chest. It is so tall, you aren't sure you'll be able to see inside of it from where you are standing. You look around and notice a staircase leading to a platform alongside the chest.

You climb the stairs which are carpeted with light gray wool. The sound of your footsteps is muffled, almost entirely silent. When you are on the platform, you see a rope tied to the lid of the chest. You reach out and pull the chest open.

Creeeaaak.

SHRIEK!

Not again. You glance around the room to make sure nothing is coming after you. When nothing happens after ten seconds, you assume you are safe. Now, you can see what is inside the chest.

You lean over the chest, extending your torch to see what is inside. At first, you can't quite tell what it is. It looks like a jumble of items. Once your brain can account for the strange shadows being cast by your torch, you gasp. It is an armor stand with a set of armor. Only, it is not the size of normal armor. It is several times larger.

Looks like that would fit an iron golem, you think. *Or maybe something even larger.*

The armor looks like it is made with gold, diamonds, and emeralds. It must be worth a fortune. When you understand what you're looking at, you break into a chuckle. Not only will it be cool to display this armor at your base, but you will be the richest player in the history of the Overworld.

You are about to loot the chest, when you feel the ground rumbling. You turn and see something rising out of the ground!

Turn the page.

You are so shocked by what you are witnessing, that you can't move. You can't even really think. You stare, unblinking, as the creature rises to its full height. It is massive. It is as large as an iron golem and then some. Its head is enormous and looks as though it has antennae on it. But, these aren't its most unusual features.

The creature's skin is the same color and pattern as the unusual spreading substance. What does that mean? It's like the creature is *made of* the substance or has learned to mimic the substance, like a massive chameleon using it for camouflage.

It is at that moment you realize something horrific: the armor you were looking at is large enough to fit on this beast! Has it emerged to stop you from stealing its armor?

The beast turns toward you. You tighten your grip on your diamond sword, but otherwise remain motionless. If it charges you, you'll think of something. The beast tilts its head side-to-side and then makes a *sculk* sound. It seems almost confused, like it doesn't know where you are. It's at that moment you realize the creature is blind. At least, it can't see with its eyes.

If it can't see you, then you should be able to escape. As much as you want the massive suit of armor, you value your life more. You descend the wool-covered stairs, glancing over your shoulder to make sure the beast isn't coming toward you. It's not.

You make it to the bottom of the stairs and step onto the deepslate floor. Your diamond boot makes a faint clicking noise. You hear the beast turn sharply and emit another *sculk* sound. It takes a few steps in your direction. *Sculk.*

You haven't moved since you heard the first *sculk* sound. It dawns on you that while the beast can't see, it can hear. And it can hear exceptionally well.

You just want to go home, but first you have to escape the beast. You can think of three possible ways to escape. Which one do you try?

If you make a dash for the door, turn to page 142.

If you stand still and hope the beast goes away, turn to page 138.

If you try to sneak out of the room, turn to page 140.

You assume that if you stand still long enough, the beast will go away. After all, it seemed as though it had been summoned by that annoying *shriek*. Maybe, if enough time passes without a shriek, it will sink back into the ground.

Your plan is logical, but an hour later, when the beast is still lingering in the room, emitting a *sculk* noise every so often, you begin to think that one of the other options is better. You can't stand still all day. Or maybe you just need a few more minutes and the beast will disappear.

If you continue to stand still, turn to page 139.
If you make a dash for the door, turn to page 142.

You hold your position for another ten minutes when suddenly your stomach growls. In the silence of the room, it sounds like a ravager's roar. The beast hears it too, emits a *sculk*, and then sprints toward you.

You make a dash for the door, but somehow the beast knows where you are heading and cuts you off. You slam into the beast. It looks at you and roars. You slash at it with your diamond sword, but it doesn't seem to do much damage.

The beast smashes you in between its two massive fists. The impact is huge. You feel as though you are on the brink of poofing. Still, you try to defeat the beast. You slash at it again, but it's no use. The beast slams its fist into your diamond chest plate and—

you poof.

If you'd like to respawn on the prior page and make a different decision, turn to page 138.

If you'd like to start at the beginning, turn to page 1.

Sneaking has to be the only viable option, right?

You study the beast for a few minutes. You are convinced that it cannot see, but can hear. It must use echolocation or something like that to locate its prey. You decide to test your theory.

You reach into your inventory and remove one of those snowballs you gathered earlier from the drop piles. You aim for the opposite side of the room. You toss the snowball. It arcs silently through the air and then splats near a soul lantern.

Sculk.

The beast emits the sound it uses to see. It snaps its head toward the area where the snowball landed and lurches in that direction. The way it lumbers, it reminds you of a massive zombie.

You wait until it gets close to the opposite wall and then take three cautious steps toward the doorway. On the third step, you hear *sculk.* The creature begins to walk in your general direction.

Can it see me? Does it know that something has changed in the room?

You stand still for two agonizing minutes until the beast wanders in another direction. You take that opportunity to toss a snowball toward the back of the room. When the snowball splats, you hear a telltale *sculk.* The beast begins to move in that direction.

You walk cautiously toward the door. Three steps. Four steps. Five—

SHRIEK!

How? Why? A block to your right has made a horrible shrieking sound. You hear the beast making *sculk* after *sculk* noise as it charges toward you.

Time to run. You make a dash for the door. Almost there.

But the beast is closing.

Just another step and—

Slam! The door snaps shut in front of you.

"What?!?"

You turn. The beast has flipped the lever on the left side of the door. It must have made the door shut.

You tense. You take a defensive stance and wield your diamond sword.

The beast approaches. You strike. The beast pounds you once and then twice.

It's over.

You poof.

If you'd like to respawn on the prior page and make a different decision, turn to page 136.

If you'd like to start at the beginning, turn to page 1.

This massive, bizarre creature makes you very nervous. If you try to stand still, you don't think you'll last more than a minute or two before freaking out. You consider trying to sneak out very slowly, but it seems like that would just prolong the agony of waiting for the beast to attack.

You decide to make a dash for the door. The beast is massive and, you assume, powerful, but its bulk might slow it down. Sure, iron golems and ravagers can move quickly sometimes, but you don't think it could be as fast as a chicken jockey.

You take a deep breath and then launch yourself toward the door. Your feet and arms pumping. The beast makes a noise. *Sculk*. Its head snaps from side-to-side.

You hear it start running. *Sculk*. That sound was closer. What if the beast is as fast as a chicken jockey?

You lean forward, hoping to increase your speed. You are almost at the doorway now. *Sculk*. Oh, wow! That was really close.

One more step, and you are past the threshold, outside of the room. You turn toward the lever you used earlier to open the door. The beast is only one or two strides from you.

"This better work," you mutter as you smack the lever up. *Sculk*.

The beast turns toward you. It knows exactly where you are. It reaches out with its hand to grab you and then the door slams shut, sealing the beast inside. At least, you hope the door is strong enough.

You hear a roar of rage from the other side of the door. Then, the beast starts to pound the door, but it doesn't budge. Whoever built that door intended on keeping the beast inside.

As you finally realize just how close you came to poofing, you begin to tremble. You decide that no treasure is worth facing that horrid creature. And, you vow to ignore any other random signs you find inside caves.

You turn away from the chamber. You retrace your path through the cave to the exit.

When you emerge on the surface of the Overworld, it is night. You spend the dark hours inside a rudimentary underground shelter.

The next morning, after an uneventful journey, you arrive at your base.

Turn to page 145.

You didn't explore the entire cave, but at least you got some useful and interesting loot. The most important of which is copper ore. You can't wait to make a fancy new roof for your base.

Still, you feel slightly ashamed for having given up before exploring the entire cave. You have a feeling there was something astonishing in its depths.

Maybe you can go back and explore it again soon.

The End

When you arrive back at your home base, you unpack your loot. You smile at the copper ore. You are eager to craft your fancy new copper roof, but you are too tired to do it today. You'll relax for the rest of the day and start crafting tomorrow.

As you eat your dinner that evening, you are thankful to be alive. That mysterious creature in the depths of the cave startled you. Actually, it freaked you out. You're not sure if you'll ever return to the depths of that cave, though you might explore its upper levels. You have a feeling there is a lot more copper ore to be found.

Later that evening, as you are drifting off to sleep, you think about the mysterious ancient city where the beast was hiding. Who built it? When? Why?

Perhaps someday, you'll solve that mystery.

The End

You never thought you'd let fear stop you from realizing any of your ambitions, but there is something about this abandoned ancient city that gives you the creeps. With a shiver and a sigh, you turn away from the lever and head for home, abandoning any chance at the treasure. It takes a long time, but eventually you arrive at the surface of the Overworld.

When you arrive back at your home base, you unpack your loot. You smile at the copper ore. You are eager to craft your fancy new copper roof, but you are too tired to do it today. You'll relax for the rest of the day and start crafting tomorrow.

Later that evening, as you are drifting off to sleep, you think about the mysterious ancient city. Who built it? When? Why? And was anything lurking behind the strange door?

Perhaps someday, you'll solve that mystery.

The End

A Note from Dr. Block

I hope you enjoyed choosing your own story with this book. I also hope you will read it over and over and have new and different adventures each time.

This is the first "craft your own adventure" book I've ever written. Would you **please leave a review** to let me know what you thought? Would you like to read more books like this? Please, let me know.

Credits: The Warden graphics are thanks to GabrielDja's warden rig for Minemator. He's got a YouTube channel, *https://www.youtube.com/channel/UCzD4VAatib6cnjils-QuuJg*, so be sure to check it out.

If you want to be alerted when I release a new book, be sure to sign up for my email list at *www.drblockbooks.com* or follow any of my social media platforms. I'm on Facebook, Twitter, and Instagram under @drblockbooks. I am also on Goodreads: just search for "Dr. Block." I recommend signing up for the newsletter because you will get TWO FREE, subscriber-exclusive short stories and a periodic newsletter.

Sincerely,

Dr. Block

More Books by Dr. Block

Craft Your Own Adventure
The Deepest Cave

Holiday Stories for Minecrafters Series:
- Valentine's Day for Baby Zeke
- Spooky Halloween Tales for Minecrafters
- A Notchmas Carol: An unofficial Minecraft holiday story inspired by Charles Dickens' A Christmas Carol (**also available in audiobook**)

The Complete Baby Zeke: Books 1-9 (**also available in audiobook**)
The Complete Baby Zeke: Books 10-12 (**also available in audiobook**)
The Complete Baby Zeke: Books 13-15 (**also available in audiobook**)

Valentine's Day for Baby Zeke

Otis: Diary of a Baby Zombie Pigman, Book 1
Otis: Diary of a Baby Zombie Pigman, Book 2: Konichi Juan
Otis: Diary of a Baby Zombie Pigman, Book 3: Training

Creeptastic (**also available in audiobook**)

Diary of a Werewolf Steve, Books 1-3

Diary of Herobrine: Origins
Diary of Herobrine: Prophecy
Diary of Herobrine: Apotheosis

Diary of a Minecraft Bat (**also available in audiobook**)

Diary of a Spider Chicken, Books 1-3

Diary of a Surfer Villager, Season One, Books 1-20
Diary of a Surfer Villager, Season Two, Books 21-30
Diary of a Surfer Villager, Season Three, Books 31-*IN PROGRESS*

The Ballad of Winston the Wandering Trader, Books 1-5 (Season One)
The Ballad of Winston the Wandering Trader, Books 6-10 (Season Two)
The Ballad of Winston the Wandering Trader, Books 11-15 (Season Three)
The Ballad of Winston the Wandering Trader, Books 16-20 (*Coming Soon*)

Tales of the Glitch Guardians, Book 1 – Origins
Tales of the Glitch Guardians, Book 2 – Kindred
Tales of the Glitch Guardians, Book 3 – Firestorm

The Ultimate Unofficial Mega Mob Mania **Coloring Book** for Minecrafters

With **Dave Villager:**
Dave the Villager and Surfer Villager: Crossover Crisis, Books 1 and 2

Writing as **Matthew Block**
Shadow Guardians—Seer